School is tough, and I don't mean the learning part. I do okay with that. But I've always had too much to say. I have trouble keeping still—big-time. Even way back in kindergarten, kids didn't like me doing frog-legged cartwheels across the little red rug and crashing through their board games. All my ideas were the loud kind. Hard to keep inside.

Every year, my teachers worked on good *strategies* for me, like:

Look at your friends when they're speaking.

Let them finish their sentences.

Listen to what they say.

I tried. I really did. But I'm not sure how well I did it. Until I met Frenchie.

LESLIE CONNOR

Anybody Here Seen Frenchie?

KATHERINE TEGEN BOOKS
An Imprint of HarperCollins Publishers

To Carey,
Thanks for always looking out for the rest of us.
With my love,
LRPC

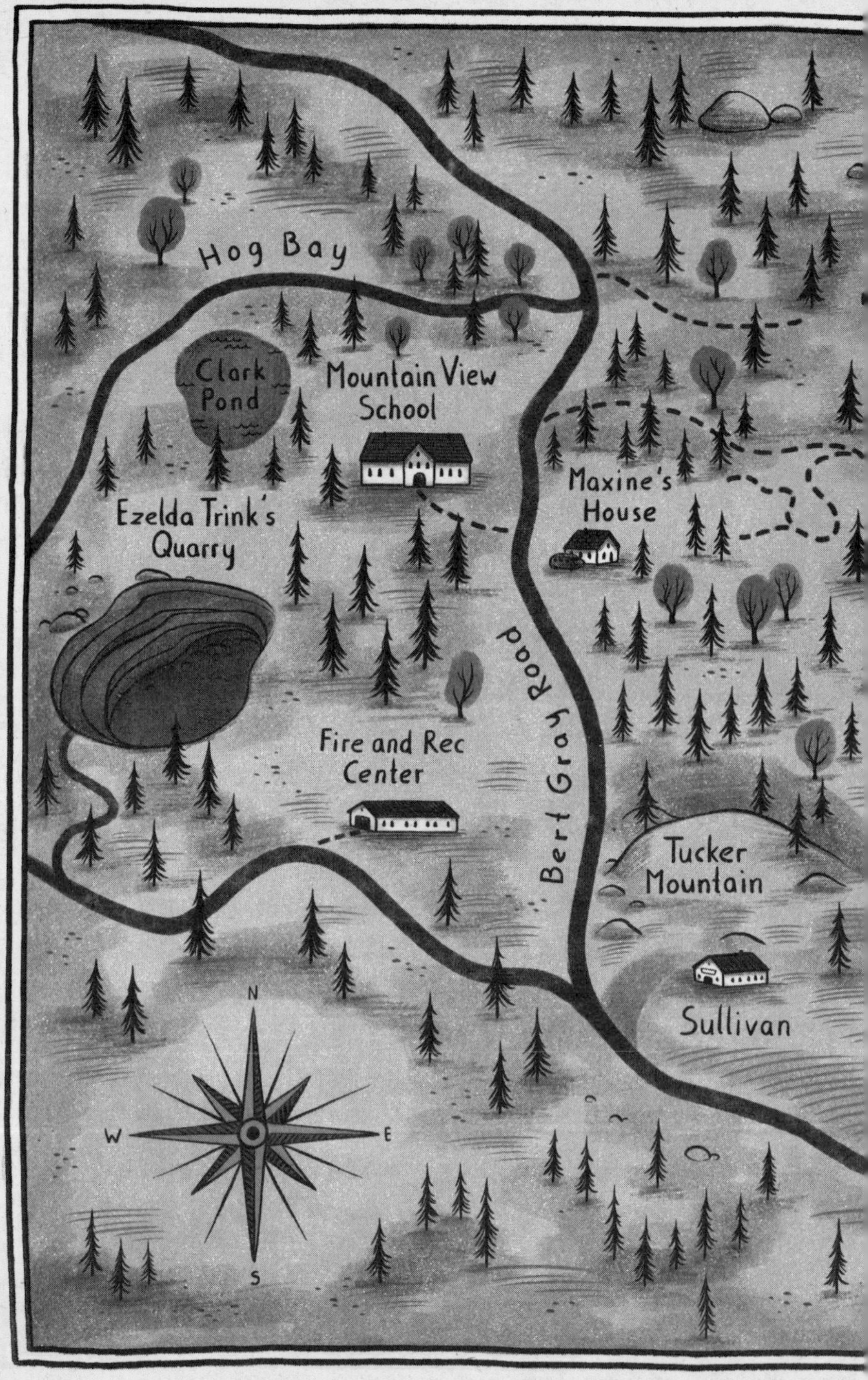

Hog Bay

Clark Pond

Mountain View School

Maxine's House

Ezelda Trink's Quarry

Bert Gray Road

Fire and Rec Center

Tucker Mountain

Sullivan

N
W   E
S

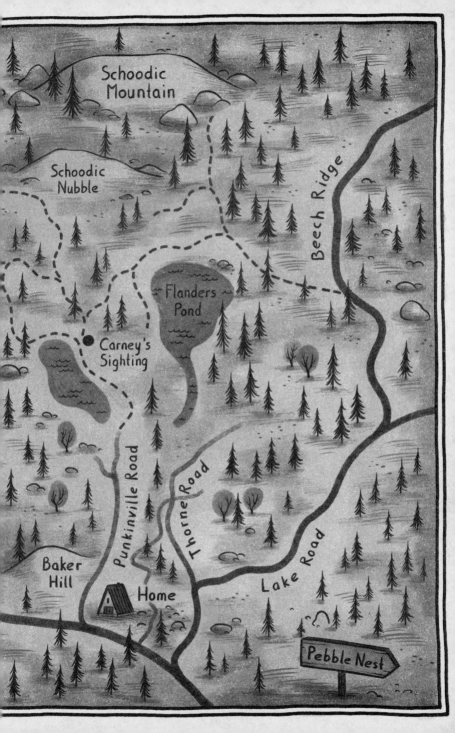

Aurora

The Letters

When our letters from the school come, we sit together on the deck at the A-frame to read them. Actually, I'll be doing all the reading.

Frenchie sits, spine straight, his freckled face tilted up. He works his fingers along the strap of the needlepoint purse he carries. In his other hand he holds his envelope. He squints and blinks at the breaks of the sun coming through the pines.

"Any birds up there?" I ask.

He doesn't answer. He never does. Not with words. But he arches his back a little.

"I saw your pine warbler early this morning," I tell him. The mention of birds is my best shot at getting his

1

attention. But it doesn't always work. It's possible I will never figure out why. But that's okay by me.

I tear into the envelope addressed to me: Aurora Pauline Petrequin.

I shake the folds out of my letter as fast as I can. "Come on, Frenchie. Open yours too!" I say. He might not get how important these letters are. But I know, our entire sixth-grade destinies are typed inside.

"Okay . . . we're about to find out who our next teacher is," I tell him. I drum the soles of my sneakers on the deck boards.

"Can you feel that? That's suspense," I say. "Here we go!" I take a huge breath and hold it while I scan the page. It takes forever to zero in, but then . . .

"Ms. Beccia!" I shout. "Yes! We're in Ms. Beccia's class! Whew!" I fan myself with my letter, then go limp where I sit. Here's what I know: Ms. Beccia is brand-new. This is a small town and the only other sixth-grade teacher is Mrs. Hillsbeck. She's been around forever, and she's *spoken to me* on the playground during recess a good number of times. Her reasons for that have all been *unreasonable*: dangerous climbing on the climber, running too close to others, handling dirt, clogging the drinking fountain with a pebble and turning it into a sprinkler, which everyone loved. Except Mrs. Hillsbeck. She got soaked trying to make it stop. She got angry too. That's some pretty bad history. There was a better place for me to spend sixth grade.

"Ms. Beccia. Yes!" I sit upright again and turn toward Frenchie. "Can I open yours now?" He is holding his envelope so lightly it's easy to take it from him.

I pick the paper triangle open. No need to drum my feet. The suspense is over. His letter will look like mine, right down to the Ms. Beccia part. "It's so great getting the new teacher," I say. "I love a fresh start."

I unfold the page which is addressed to Nathan French Livernois. Makes me snort because nobody ever calls him Nathan. I clear my throat.

"Okay." I work my way down the page. What I see makes me quiet. (I am not a quiet girl.) I reread it. I look at Frenchie. He's still staring up into the branches.

"What the heck?" I whisper. I let the letter fall into my lap. Then I yell, "What the heck! How's that going to work?" I jump to my feet and run in through the open door of the A-frame calling, "Mom! Pop! Gracia! There's a mess-up of all mess-ups here! Frenchie and I got put in different classes!"

Aurora

The First Time We Met Jewell Laramie and I Tried to Play Softball

Mom and Pop are as surprised as I am about Frenchie being in one sixth-grade classroom and me being in the other. Pop even called the school to make sure the assignments are right. (They are.) They all tell me it will work out fine. Frenchie and I will still take the bus together. We'll see each other at lunch and on the playground.

Mom says things like: "Remember, Aurora, there was a time before Frenchie lived here and you survived just fine."

I say things like: "Yeah! That was three years ago! I'm not used to that anymore! And what about Frenchie? Can we agree that there is a little bit more to this than just two friends getting separated? Can we?"

I remember the summer before Frenchie and Gracia came. That was the year I tried playing softball, which I only did because the coach came to our house to recruit me. And it was a chance to play *something* with other kids. I already knew I had a darn-good throwing arm. That comes from me being a rock hound.

I don't have much of a collection. Yet. I am particular. I'm searching for tourmaline. Parts of Maine offer great gem hunting. I'd give up sour pickles for a month to go digging for minerals over in Oxford or Androscoggin. That's where the old mica mines are, and the really cool pegmatites. Those are veins of igneous rock, and that's where you find the good stuff like beryl, topaz, *and* tourmaline.

Around home, I pick up rocks all the time. They're mostly granite, and I have collected enough of that. I throw them far as I can so I don't refind them. Why let a rock disappoint you twice? Pop says the lack of tourmaline in our part of Maine (fact) could be my ticket to the majors (joke). He says my arm gets stronger every time I *don't* find a piece of the good stuff, which is, so far, all the time. I like choosing targets. Mostly boulders so I don't hurt the trees—or anything else. Underhand, overhand, I've got good aim, and I can put enough speed on a rock to make it zing.

Our town has a girls' softball league, and Coach Jewell

Laramie wants every girl in town to play. That's why she came to see me. She thought we were new here because the A-frame was newly finished. The door was open because of the stinky new paint smell, and because Mom and Pop were bringing in the kitchen cupboards that day. Jewell called hello. Then she walked right in and thunked a hunk of something frozen all wrapped in plastic on our kitchen table.

"Hey, neighbors! I'm Jewell Laramie." She tipped her cap, which looked to be trapping a pouf of pale golden hair.

"I'm Aurora. Aurora Pauline Petrequin," I told her.

"Ah! Just the girl I'm looking for," said Jewell.

That was an even bigger surprise than seeing her sweep into our new house. I waited while Mom and Pop introduced themselves—Rene and Ed—and pronounced our last name twice over.

"Brought you folks some dinner!" Jewell nodded toward the hunk in the bag. "Venison tenderloin," she added.

"Oh, we don't eat that," I said. "That's deer meat. Deer are mammals. We don't eat mammals."

Jewell looked at Mom and Pop. "Oh. Tells it like it is, does she?" She cocked her head in my direction.

"She does," said Mom, and Pop nodded.

"If it makes you feel any different, there was no suffering. I took this deer during bow season. Had a clean, double-lung shot. The only shot I'll take."

Clean, double-lung shot.

How can that *not* cause suffering? I looked at the package on our table and thought about pointing out that it was dead.

"We appreciate the gesture," Pop said.

"Doesn't offend me," Jewell said, "and I hope I haven't offended you."

"You haven't, and we don't mean to be ungracious," Pop explained.

"But we still don't eat that," I repeated. "Oh. That sounds ungracious, doesn't it?"

"A little bit," Mom said.

I looked at Jewell. "I blurt things. I do that a lot," I told her.

"Nothing wrong with honesty. I like it," Jewell said. "Tell me, what do you eat?"

"We say feather, fin, and flora," Pop told her. "Local dairy and a little seafood."

"Yut, yut . . ." (Some Mainers will say *yut* instead of *yes*.) Jewell Laramie nodded like she was really paying attention. So when she started to tell us all about her girls' softball league, I listened to her. She practically begged me to come play.

"All levels are welcome, and U-eight is all about learning the game and having a good time," she said. "Think about it, Aurora. I bet there's an athlete in you." She picked up her frozen deer meat, held it under her arm, and gave it a pat. "You folks should know . . . hunters are a fact of life in Maine."

"Acknowledged," said Pop. "We aren't new to Maine."

"Yeah, I've been here all my life," I said.

"And I've been here half of mine," Pop added.

"And about a third for me," Mom said. "We're not even new to town. Just new to this spot."

"Yeah, we moved out of our house on the bay, and now we rent it out to folks from away," I said. (If you are from away, it means you don't live in Maine; you are a visitor.) "And maybe you saw that little house right next door here?" I pointed. "We're going to rent that one out too."

"Gotcha," said Jewell, and she put up her thumb, which had one of those purple nails on it. Like she'd whacked it with a hammer or pinched it in a wood splitter, probably months before. There's something about a purple thumb like that—always makes me like the person who's got it. Enough to go try playing ball.

But, sheeshy-sheesh! That game is full of rules, and you stand around that diamond for hours and nothing happens. Ugh. Then if someone finally does hit a ball and you decide to run across the diamond to stop it, your own teammate by the name of Darleen Dombroski could decide to *cry* because you got in her way on the play. And stepped on her ankle. And gave it an accidental grinding. Never mind you made a perfect throw to first base and

8

got the hitter out—*which I did*. That night Darleen got her mother to call my mother. (Darleen's mother has been calling my mother since we were in kindergarten.) This time, Mrs. Dombroski told Mom that there are *positions* in softball, and that maybe she could help her daughter (me) understand that so no one else would get hurt.

Well, Coach Jewell tried playing me everywhere. Not like a punishment. She tries everyone everywhere. She rotated me to the outfield, where there was *less than nothing* to do—except handstands. I pulled my glove off and kicked my feet into the air. I tried cartwheels next, and I figured out the cool trick of pulling up grass on the way over. Then throwing it like confetti.

Coach Jewell leaned out of the dugout, calling, "Aurora! Aurora P.! No gymnastics out there! Be ready! A hit could come your way."

"Yeah, I won't hold my breath about that," I called back. "I could take a nap out here." I faked a yawn, but it turned into a real one—noisy too. Some of my teammates giggled. They snorted and covered their faces with their gloves. "I could grow a year older waiting out here . . . am I nine yet? Am I ten?"

But before the game was over, my teammates, who were also my classmates at school, started to whisper that I was "not funny" and "so annoying." They were tired of me, and I was tired of softball.

Jewell Laramie came to the house the next day.

She brought us a brook trout. She set it down and said, "Feather, fin, and flora, correct? Well, here's some *fin*!" Then she showed me how the game of softball works by putting all our mugs and the salt and pepper shakers on the table in a diamond. She said *teamwork* at least five times. I propped my chin on the table and tried not to interrupt.

Finally, I said, "Coach, I know all that." Because I did. "But it takes way too long for something to happen. I can't stand it. I need more to do!"

Jewell looked me over a second. She nodded and said something nice about me and my raw talent. Mom gave Jewell a bag of apricot muffins. Muffins for brook trout. Like, all good. We're friends. But my days on the softball diamond were done.

I didn't miss it. Plenty of rocks to inspect and throw, and that's what I did pretty much all summer long. On my own. I didn't have my little brother, Cedar, yet, and I was the only kid living on our road. But that was about to change.

Aurora

Mainstreaming Frenchie

The first time I met Frenchie Livernois we were waiting for the bus at the end of the long driveway we share. That was three years ago. Third grade.

I ran, jumped, and hopped all the way there, rip-ready for the first day of school. Another whole summer gone, and now the bus was coming to get me again. I *loved* going places. Still do.

In fact, we'd just come back to Maine after a vacation with Gram and Gramp in Connecticut. That's why we weren't around to see our new neighbors move into the little house beside the A-frame. But Pop had said there was going to be a mom and a kid living there. A change like that is pretty big news where we live.

I remember feeling my heart leap when I spotted them at the end of the drive. I ran and skidded to a stop right next to the woman and sprayed little stones over her clogs and against her bare ankles. Mom pulled me back.

"Careful, Aurora," she said.

"Oops! Sorry! Sorry!" I said.

Our new neighbor was nice. She laughed and her brown curls bounced. I waited for the boy to laugh too. But he stood a few yards away from us, back turned, almost like he hadn't heard us come up at all. Weird, I thought.

I wanted to get to him, but his mom was talking to my mom, and I was working on being a good listener. Sort of my life project. She explained that her name was Gracia, and that her boy's name was Nathan French Livernois. But she had called him Frenchie from the day he was born.

There we go, I thought, because if she had not explained, I was going to have to ask about that name.

"I'm Aurora Pauline Petrequin," I said. I bopped from side to side and gave myself a knock on the head. "That's *Pet-ruh-quin*, just so you know. It's easy. But nobody gets it right. They say *Ped-a-guin*. And *Peterkin*. Pfft! Every year, I have to tell my new teacher, sound it out!"

"You would think they could do that," said Gracia. Total twinkle in her eye.

Mom stood behind me, her hands cupped loosely on my shoulders.

"Anyway, you can call me plain *Aurora*," I said, and I

roared my name to be friendly, and because Aurora is a name that likes to be roared, *and* I thought if I was loud enough that boy Frenchie might turn around.

Gracia leaned down and smiled. "I'm going to guess that there's nothing plain about you." She had a voice like butter.

"You might be right," I said. Then I skittered away from the moms and went over to Frenchie. Who in this world doesn't turn around to say hello? I shuffled up beside him. I took a good look at all his edges—his pro-file—and the way his dark hair was trimmed around his ear. His skin was light like seashells and sprinkled with summer freckles.

"Hey. I'm Aurora," I roared, but not too loudly. "Good to meet ya," I said.

Frenchie stared straight ahead.

"Hellooo?" I tried again. He didn't answer. I knew plenty of kids in town who were not too interested in me. But, sheeshy-sheesh, this was a brand-new one. Wasn't he even going to give me a try? I leaned in. "We're neighbors now, ya know."

That boy did not move.

I walked all the way around him. Took a good look at those tan pants of his. He had them pulled way up, belted so tight his plaid button-down shirt puffed out almost like a costume. That's all he has ever worn, for as long as I've known him.

Frenchie Livernois: plaid mushroom. I stood beside him. Tried to stare at whatever he was staring at. Was it our mailboxes on that post across the road? Something in the field? Maybe he'd seen something crawling around in the ditch.

"You know," I said, "there's a wood rat that travels along there. You like animals?"

Frenchie's elbows straightened by his sides. His hands twitched. Then stopped. He didn't quit staring, except to blink his long dark eyelashes—like slow motion.

"Wood rat." I said it again just to see if he'd move. Nope.

I spun on one foot, grinding the gravel. I leaped and landed in a lunge, arms wide, right into the middle of Mom and Gracia's conversation.

"Hey! What's with him?" I blurted. I pointed my finger behind me.

Mom said, "Aurora, try not to—"

"Interrupt," I said. "Yeah, sorry about that. But what the heck?" I jabbed my finger back toward the boy again.

Gracia smiled. She used her butter voice again. "Oh, Aurora, I was telling your mom, Frenchie doesn't talk. Not in words. But he does hear you."

I pulled my chin back. "Oh. Hears me, huh?" I wasn't so sure. Not that I thought she was lying. But I wondered if she was one of those moms who would say the thing she

14

wanted to think was true even when it wasn't. Like Darleen Dombrowski's mom who kept saying all through second grade that Darleen was "a kind and patient soul."

I had news for her. Even way back then.

Darleen is a difficult acquaintance of mine. I'm not alone there. Other kids don't play with her, and since they don't play with me either, the school has been trying to pair us up for years. Exhausting is what that is. Unsuccessful too.

But I was heading into third grade that very morning. Fresh start coming up. I had my *strategies*. For one, I was aiming to do less blurting. (I aim for that every year.) It's tricky for me. Pop says I should be me, and that people learn by living and doing. Trouble is, I end up having to *undo* a lot of stuff that I mess up.

Anyway, I went up to Frenchie that first morning and stood close to his ear. "Sh-should be here s-s-soon," I told him. I put those *s*'s right into his ear. "The bus-s-s, that iz-z-z . . ." He twitched and pulled his shoulder up. Kept staring. I stepped back. His mom was right. He could hear. He was also ear ticklish.

"I bet you don't get in trouble, do ya?" I said, watching those eyelashes again.

I took two giant Mother-May-I steps toward the road and looked. Still no bus, which meant I had time to scratch open a few of my Connecticut-vacation mosquito

15

bites. Or maybe they were from when we'd made a pit stop in Massachusetts. I started counting off the states we'd driven through on our way home the day before. So I was thinking about states when I heard Frenchie's mom tell my mom, "So, I decided to bring him here, where I could *Maine stream* him."

I quit digging my skin. I popped straight up. I looked at that woman hard. Was she saying she'd moved here to Maine and was going to put Frenchie in a stream?

"Well, hey," I called. "Can he swim?"

Mom and Gracia both laughed.

Mom said, "Mainstream means Frenchie's going to attend public school and go to class like you, Aurora."

Gracia Livernois said, "But you ask a good question. Frenchie doesn't swim."

"Uh, well, knowing how to swim is a smart idea for anyone living around here," I said. "We've got a place where we can teach him."

Gracia knotted her hands together. She brought them up under her chin. "I want him to learn," she said. Then she added, "So many things."

She seemed hunched up and nervous, like she was worried about all the streams in Maine, and the ponds and the ocean too. But I get it now. It was more than that. She had a no-talk boy, heading off for a new start at a new school in a new town.

16

Frenchie

She Was Aurora

Frenchie Livernois stared at the field beyond the mail-boxes. Birds were there. Low, in tall grass.

The girl came up from behind. Running, spinning, jumping. She landed beside him. She spoke at him.

"*Wood rat.*"

Quiet is good for seeing birds. So Frenchie kept watch, while the girl hissed right into the hole of his ear.

She told him, "*S-s-soon,*" and "*Bus-s-s.*"

The girl's voice was one. Single. Clear. It gave Frenchie the feeling of birds without seeing birds. Lightness in his fingers. It moved inside him on the path up his arms. Down his ribs. It made his shoulder inch up. A tug from somewhere inside him.

Pretty soon he knew she was Aurora.

She looked where he looked. At the field. When the birds flew up, Aurora called. "Whew-a whew-wheee! Did ya know those were there, all this time, Frenchie?" She flapped her arms.

Arms are like wings. They are not wings.

Hands are like wings. They are not wings.

Frenchie watched the birds put dark flicker shapes on the pale sky. They drew loops, then grew small as dots.

When the birds were gone, Frenchie flapped his hands. He meant to make birdsong. He thought he had. But there was a rumble—down-road from where he stood. It juddered the bottoms of his feet. He felt it at his middle.

Aurora called. Her one clear voice.

"Frenchie! It's coming! *Bus-s-s-s!*"

She was Aurora. And Frenchie was going with her.

Aurora

The Special Person

I remember Mom sticking a bunch of dot Band-Aids on my bites right before the bus came. (She still carries them in all her pockets.) She gave me a quick hug (because I don't like long ones), and I followed Frenchie onto the bus. He proved again that he could hear. How else would he have known what our driver, Helene (same one I had since kindergarten), meant when she told him to take that nice seat right behind her?

"And where do you want me?" I asked.

"Aurora, *baby*, sit anywhere you'd like." (Helene calls everyone *baby*. She draws it out real long, like, *baaaay-bee*.)

The bus was full of the kids who were always splitting off to make tight circles of themselves at school. And at the playground. And at the town beach every summer.

I picked the seat across the aisle from Frenchie. I waved to Mom with both arms, and she waved back with one because she had the other around Gracia's shoulders. Those two were going back to our house for coffee before work, and to become best friends.

I liked being back on the bus. I liked the smell of the rubber floor mats, and I loved the jiggly ride. I liked kicking my Band-Aid-dotted legs out in front of me and wiggling my butt to make the seat squeak. I liked humming a hum that was not a real song, and shouting up to Helene to ask how her summer was, and did she see that cat at the side of the road just now? How about that tractor tire full of black-eyed Susans in that yard right there? Was she surprised I didn't live at the beach anymore?

I liked feeling as if the year was new. No mistakes yet. When I looked over at Frenchie, he seemed pretty much the same as when he'd been staring off across the end of our road at the mailboxes, but now he was staring out the window. Made me wonder, does this kid know what new is? Does he feel that? Does he care? If I watch him real close will I be able to tell?

When we got to school, there was a classroom aide there to meet him, right off the bus. That was Mrs. Kingsley.

"He doesn't talk," I said. "Hope somebody told you that."

"Yes, Aurora. Thank you," she said. "Here we go. This way!" She was very cheery. She marched Frenchie Livernois down the hall with one hand on his back. I didn't think he liked that. He kept hurrying forward and scooting over. I ran up to try to tell Mrs. Kingsley that she should maybe stop doing that, and I accidentally stepped on her heel.

"Ouch!" she said, and she hopped twice.

"Sorry!"

Frenchie was hauling ahead of us. Mrs. Kingsley hustled after him.

Turned out we were all going to Mr. Ritter's room. Frenchie was going to be in my class.

The best thing about the first minutes of the first day of school is nothing has gone wrong yet. I bolted into that room to see if I could find kids to match up with. Like, get a spot at their table. That's always kind of hard for me. *Trying* to fit in does not work. It means folding yourself up into some shape that doesn't feel like you.

School is tough, and I don't mean the learning part. I do okay with that. But I've always had too much to say. I have trouble keeping still—big-time. Even way back in kindergarten, kids didn't like me doing frog-legged cartwheels across the little red rug and crashing through their board games. All my ideas were the loud kind. Hard to keep inside.

Every year, my teachers worked on good *strategies* for me, like:

Look at your friends when they're speaking.

Let them finish their sentences.

Listen to what they say.

I tried. I really did. At home, Mom and Pop tried to help too. They always said, "First things first, Aurora: you get to be who you are. Everyone does. The trick is to see if part of you can take a little time. Watch other people, and see if you can tell how they feel. Be aware."

I actually like that idea. But I'm not sure how well I did it. Until I met Frenchie. I did watch him. The great part was, he didn't care if I talked my head off while I was at it. You can do that; you can talk and watch at the same time. But I've noticed that it works better if I am quiet every once in a while.

The kids in our third-grade class watched Frenchie the first day. Stared at him, is what I mean. Probably wondering what was up with him, same way I did when I met him at the bus stop. I guess nobody was used to a kid who didn't talk and who seemed to like birds more than humans. He looked into the trees a lot. He flapped his hands like little wings, and it turned out he had a mess of bird pictures stuffed into his backpack. But kids stared at Frenchie, then looked away before they had to say anything. Then they stopped noticing him at all. That's what I saw. They leaned left or right to talk around him. They rushed past him to get to one another. Like he wasn't there. Frenchie Livernois. Invisible boy.

But for me, something started to happen those first weeks of third grade. Every time I turned around, there was Frenchie, right behind me. Staring. Not at me. Just at whatever. But he stayed near. Our families were spending time together at home, and like I say, our moms are best friends.

One day, Mrs. Kingsley said, "You do very well with Frenchie, Aurora."

"So do you," I said. It was true. She had stopped rushing him down the hallway. She'd quit putting her hand on his shoulder.

"Well, thank you. But what I mean is, you're very good at reading his behavior."

"What's that mean?" I asked. "You mean seeing how he feels?"

"Exactly," she said. "I think he's chosen you. You are Frenchie's special person."

I smiled. "Yeah. I am."

Aurora

Pebble Nest

Pebble Nest belongs to us. That's our big old house on Flanders Bay. Not fancy. Just awesome. The place can sleep ten people as long as they like each other. If you do two cartwheels down the lawn, then jump the scruffy hedge, you will wind up on a half-circle beach that is covered with a bazillion smooth pebbles, all colors and all kinds of rock. Pop always says there's no better spot for a salty swim and a nap in the sun.

We used to live there. Now we have the A-frame in the woods and we rent Pebble Nest out by the week from May to October. Mom and Pop say the money helps butter our bread. I say Pebble Nest is a reason to love Saturdays.

That's when it's ours again. Saturdays from 10:30 a.m. to 2:30 p.m.

There is a price to pay. We have to clean. The whole place. From top to bottom. Some people wouldn't like the work of it. But it's different when you love a place. Besides, we go at it like machines. We're almost always done by noon. (Best thing we ever did was buy doubles of all the linens so we can take the washing home and bring it back clean the next week.) Then, as long as the weather is even close to good, we can hit the beach to swim, hunt for rocks, or dig for clams. We have lunch up on the lawn. Feels like we live there again. We pack up at two thirty because there has to be no trace of us by three, when the next renters arrive. Sometimes it's families. Sometimes it's a bunch of yoga people or watercolor artists. It's always people from away.

Frenchie comes to Pebble Nest with us every week now, without his mom. But it didn't start out like that. The whole first year, Gracia came too, and she barely let Frenchie out of her sight. Gracia helped us learn to watch him, to *see* all the different ways Frenchie can be. He can get upset. Not often, and he's not a tantrum kid. But if he gets overwhelmed, he shuts down. He tucks up on the ground and wraps his arms over his head. Gets me right in the heart. But Gracia says it's Frenchie's way of claiming the space he needs to get through the upset. The best strategy is to catch it before it happens. But if it does, we let Frenchie know that we are there for him. I think he gets that.

Frenchie's comfortable with us. For two summers now he's been showing up at the door to the A-frame every Saturday morning, ready to go to Pebble Nest.

"It's nice for us and nice for Gracia," Mom says. "It isn't easy being a single parent."

I get that. Pretty sure all parents like breaks. Gracia beams when she sees Frenchie hop out of our van at the end of a Saturday. She gets him back again, and it's like her boy is all her eyes can see. Makes me smile even when I'm not thinking about smiling.

I love it that Frenchie comes to Pebble Nest. He helps! He knows to take the bin full of recycling out to our van. He slides the empty bin under the kitchen sink, right where it belongs. There are some things Frenchie gets. Can't tell you why.

In the upstairs bedrooms, I play tornado. I whip the sheets off the beds and spin the pillows right out of the cases. Frenchie piles the linens into the basket. I always take a few bounces on the naked mattresses. The twin beds are great for a back-and-forth. Of course, I'm not supposed to do that. Frenchie sees me. But he'd never rat me out. When the beds are done, we dust. He's not the best at it, but he follows behind me with his own cloth. Good enough.

The beach at Pebble Nest is where we taught Frenchie how to swim. We got right on that, like Gracia wanted. Mom knew what to do. She said Frenchie should learn two things first: to hold his breath underwater and to float on his back and breathe. The beach was perfect because he could wade into the chilly water nice and easy. I was super excited. I wanted to splash like a sea lion. But I kept calm for Frenchie, and Gracia too. We walked him out just far enough that all we had to do was bend our knees and lower ourselves underwater. I did all the demonstrating.

"Breathing place!" I said, stretching my arms high. Then I pointed down and said, "No breathing below." I took a breath and lowered myself under. It felt like baby steps. But then one Saturday, Frenchie did like I did. He went under! He never choked, not once. I laughed at the way he kept his eyes open, even in the salty water. He was mostly a stare-at-nothing boy, but it seemed like Frenchie looked right at me whenever he was coming up for air. When he did the same with Gracia, she didn't just laugh, she cried.

Teaching him to float was harder. I'm not sure the idea of lying down on top of the water made sense to him, even though I showed him a hundred times. "Sit back, then lie back." Even with Mom and Gracia on each side of him and their good old mom hands underneath him, he would not lie back. He kept *sitting*.

"Sheeshy-sheesh! Way to give yourself a good dunking!" I said.

Our skin was starting to wrinkle. Frenchie's lips were blue. He shivered. I watched him sit back and sink one more time. Enough, I thought. Time to warm up in the sun.

The sun!

"Oh! Wait! I got it," I said. "Frenchie, watch me." I motioned Mom and Gracia out of the way.

"Aurora, he's been watching you," Mom said.

"He's been staring," I said. "Frenchie. Look, look." I tilted my face up. "Are ya watching? Do you know what I feel right now? The sun. On my face. It's up there. You know it is. Now I'm going to sit a little, then I'm going to *lie* back. And I'm going to keep the sun on my face. I'm going to rest my whole self on the water." I slowly lay back. With my ears underwater and my eyes half-closed, I told him, "Here I am just lying on the water. Relaxing. Breathing. And there's the sun up there. Betcha I'll see a bird fly by. That's right, a bird! You've gotta try this, Frenchie."

Well, he did it. Face tilted up to the sun, he lay back and made his body straight.

"That's it, Frenchie! Relax and breathe."

He floated and floated, while Mom and Gracia and I clapped our hands and celebrated.

If there is one thing Frenchie loves as much as birds, it is the sun.

Aurora

Two Years Ago:
When Cedar Came Home

With Frenchie and Gracia right next door, it was like our family got bigger. That first winter, I asked Pop if we could build a covered bridge to connect the little house to the A-frame. He said Frenchie and I should build it out of snow, and we tried. There was a melt before we finished. But when more snow came—and we can get dumped on here—Pop cleared a path with the snowblower, from our door to Frenchie's door. We must have gone back and forth ten times a day. We had two places to get a cup of cocoa.

When my little brother, Cedar, came along the next fall, Gracia and Frenchie helped like family would help.

Cedar was adopted, and that can take way longer than it takes to grow a baby. I mean, years. Mom and Pop couldn't have any more kids after me, so there was nothing to do but sign papers and wait. Forever. But, funny how one day when we weren't expecting it, the call came, and boy, did we hop to it. Mom and Pop got in the car, and I went to stay the night with Gracia and Frenchie. In the morning, we came back to the A-frame. We cleaned and washed up my old baby clothes and some of Frenchie's too. We hung the crib sheets in the sun. I was glad the three of us were together because I was worried. We had gotten ready for our new baby a few times before. And then . . . no baby. All of us cried. We felt like someone was missing.

But this time, Mom and Pop came home with our Cedar.

Here's what I remember about that afternoon:

First, our baby was crying his head off. He was pulling at his ears and leaving little bloody kitten scratches on his cheeks. "Poor little man," Mom said. "He's got double ear infections."

Second, he had shiny black curls all over his head that lay down like little *o*'s.

Third, even though he was not as weensie as the newborns I had seen, he was still the smallest, twisty-squirmy little person I'd ever held in my arms.

The fourth thing I remember was how I felt way deep

inside the middle of me. I decided it had to be my heart melting. That made me laugh and then cry, and look at my parents, then back at Cedar, and laugh again. I knew I was going to love that screaming baby for the rest of my life.

Cedar had fevers and misery for the whole first winter and on into mud season. He stayed up way past everyone's bedtime. He needed a lot of rocking, humming, and dancing with Mom and Pop, and even me. Frenchie and his mom came every day. Gracia would dance Cedar all around the open floor plan of the A-frame while Frenchie and I listened to bird calls at the computer and Mom and Pop took naps.

Cedar saw our pediatrician a lot. He sucked down syringes full of gloppy pink medicine. Then he threw it up and magically made it look like twice as much.

Mom and Pop took him to an ear doctor, and a man called the naturopath, and a woman called an acupuncturist. Finally, finally, summertime came and the ear troubles faded, at least for a while. It was like Cedar could start being Cedar. Mom and Pop think the warm, dry weather did it. Probably right. He had troubles again last winter. The infections come and go now. Not as bad. Still, we know there are times when Cedar doesn't hear us. The doctor said that might be why he doesn't talk much yet, and why he's hard to understand. The words probably sound right to him. They just aren't always clear to us. But he tries, so we try too. We listen. This year, Cedar finally calls me by my name. He says, *Awoh-wah*. And I love it.

Aurora

Darleen Dombroski

At Mountain View School, we celebrate new siblings. (I think it's nice that they say *new siblings*, because sometimes older kids are new too.)

Ever since kindergarten I have been meeting everybody else's new siblings, mostly tiny babies. I had to get to fourth grade before it was finally my turn. I was rip-ready to introduce my baby brother. Turned out to be the best day of school ever.

Mrs. Santiago had our class measure Cedar in inches. Then we converted him to metric. We had a talk about adoption. We sang "You Are My Sunshine" and "What a Wonderful World." We ate cupcakes in Cedar's honor, and I got to take one home for our freezer. Cedar could have it when Mom and Pop decided he was old enough. At the end, we set up for a photograph of all of us together. I sat in the center holding Cedar, and my classmates crowded all around us. I looked left, then right.

"Wait, wait! Where's Frenchie?" I wanted to know. He'd gotten inched out—all the way to one end, almost out of the shot. "Make way! Frenchie to the front!" I called.

Mrs. Santiago brought him up beside me. "This is our picture," I told him. "You, me, and this new baby bird." I rocked Cedar in my arms. We got the shot.

The next morning, Mrs. Santiago gave me two prints of the photo. "The large one in the frame is for your family," she said. "I laminated the smaller one for you, Aurora. Pocket-size, so you can carry it with you."

I thanked her, then I spun around the room, showing the picture to anyone who wanted to see it. During class, I put my picture into my desk, where I could sneak peeks at it. But Mrs. Santiago had to ask if maybe the photo was too great a distraction for me.

"Last time," I promised her. I pushed it into the back of my desk. Before lunch and recess, I put that photo in the pocket of my shorts.

Every day, Frenchie and I run, from the edge of the blacktop, across the playing field to the backstop. It's a fifty-yard dash according to our gym teacher. Of course we run back again, so it's really a hundred.

But this day, our art teacher, Mrs. Chandra, had put

out a big new bucket of sidewalk chalk. That always brings a swarm of artists. I couldn't resist. I grabbed a thick new stick of chalk and claimed a patch of blacktop.

Frenchie paced beside me. He went twenty feet away, then came back, again and again. I knew he wanted to run. He counts on things to happen the same way every day.

"One quick chalk picture," I told him. "Okay?" Then I heard a voice I knew.

"He doesn't know what you're saying."

I scraped the tip of my chalk down hard. *Darleen Dombroski.* If I had noticed that she was making chalk pictures too, I would have skipped it. (One of my strategies at school is to stay clear of Darleen. I came up with that one on my own.)

"He does know," I said. "Look at his hands." I waited for her to put eyes on Frenchie. Emma Bowman and Milo Robinette looked up from their chalk art too, and I figured, good. They will notice him. "See him making those little fist squeezes?" I asked.

"So what?" Darleen shrugged.

"That's what he does when something isn't quite right. Like now. He's impatient. And disappointed. He wants me to run with him."

Darleen huffed and shook her head. She swung her shoulders. *No, no, no.*

"He might be a little upset that we are talking *about* him instead of *to* him. Or he might not like the way you're talking to me," I added. "Just saying."

"You don't know that. You're not his mind reader, Aurora."

That made me think back to third grade, when Mrs. Kingsley said I was good at reading Frenchie's behavior. I watched the different ways he stood, and moved his hands, and fluttered his eyelids. Those things told me what his mind was up to and how he was feeling. So . . . maybe I *was* Frenchie's mind reader. To me, it was funny! I tried to hold back a snicker, but it flew out anyway— snort! That made Milo laugh. Then Emma laughed too. Darleen narrowed her eyes at me.

Frenchie swept by again, still squeezing his hands open and closed.

"Hey, I'm trying to draw a cardinal for you," I said. "But this red chalk is more like pink. . . ."

Then I remembered the photo in my pocket. Frenchie would love to hold it for me. I jumped up. "Hey, want to look?" I held the photo out. He put his hand up to take it, then paced away again, all one motion. "It's from our Sibling Day!" I called.

"He won't remember *Sibling Day*." Darleen bobbled her head as she spoke. "He definitely doesn't get that the baby is your brother. Your baby *bird*," she added, *not nicely*. That's when I should have walked away from Darleen. But in the next second Frenchie came striding up with the photo in his hand. He was looking at it closely, the same way he studies his bird pictures. So I had to go and say it:

"Hey, Darleen. Check it out," I waved my chalk stick in Frenchie's direction. "See how he's looking at that photo? He knows every person in it, including Cedar."

"You can't be sure. . . ."

"Well . . . when Frenchie is at our house, which is almost every day, he's the first one to hear Cedar fussing when he wakes up. He goes and stands beside the crib until someone comes to get Cedar."

"Proves nothing," Darleen said.

"It proves everything!"

Then Emma Bowman piped up. "Well, it sounds like he knows there is a baby. And he pays attention to him." Then Milo Robinette agreed.

Then it got quiet. And then . . . there it was, Darleen's crumpled face. The cry. This is the tough thing about her. The inside of her head tells her that everything is somehow *mean to Darleen*. There had been plenty of times her crying didn't go so well for *me*. So I jumped in.

"Don't cry!" I said. "If you don't believe me, fine. Forget it."

She sniffled and whimpered. (I can't stand when she does that.) Both Emma and Milo got up and patted her back. "It's okay, Darleen. You're fine."

Mrs. Woodsum, who had recess duty that day, came

over. Darleen's voice shook while she told Mrs. Woodsum that I told a made-up story—*lied*—to make her feel bad. *And* laughed at her!

"Nope. Not a lie." I pushed my hands deep into my pockets. "It was a true story. An example, actually. And the laugh was just—a noise that came out of me."

Frenchie stood behind me, clenching the Sibling Day photo in one hand and making fist squeezes with his other.

Emma and Milo and some other kids—ones who don't play with me, or Frenchie, *or* Darleen—actually stood up for me. First time ever for that.

Mrs. Woodsum walked Darleen over to the corner of the blacktop, and I don't know what got said there. She told me to wait. I was next. I folded my arms on my chest. Frenchie stood beside me, in his full *no* pose now, chin jutting.

"Hey, Frenchie. It's okay," I said. "Just taking a bite out of recess, is all." I sighed. "Forget the chalk. We should be running our hundred-yard dash."

When Mrs. Woodsum took me to the corner, I told her exactly what had happened. "So you can see," I said, "Darleen was *terribly confused and wrong*." Mrs. Woodsum walked me back to Darleen. She held us both by a hand—firm but gentle, which is infuriating—and she said, "Now, girls, Frenchie doesn't speak, but he is a human being just like each of you are. So let's always choose kindness, okay?"

What? Was she really saying that to me?

"Girls? Do you both understand?"

Darleen nodded, but I shrugged.

"Aurora?" Mrs. Woodsum pressed me.

"I am kind to Frenchie," I said. I twisted my hand out of Mrs. Woodsum's hand. "I should *not* be in trouble right now—"

"Aurora. You're not in trouble." Mrs. Woodsum sure sounded stern. "Remember that there's always something to learn from every disagreement."

I disagree, I thought. But I didn't say it.

"Can I go now? Please?"

Mrs. Woodsum said yes. I tossed my chalk back in the bucket.

"Frenchie! Time to run! Ready, set, go!"

Aurora

Back-to-School Shopping

Mom and Gracia are sticking to all our back-to-school traditions. They know it's bugging me that Frenchie and I won't be together.

Mom's a freelance writer. Most of her articles are for the *Great-State Travel Guide of Maine*. (There is a *Great-State Travel Guide of New Hampshire* too. And Vermont. Et cetera.) She makes space in her days by writing at night. She promises that we'll go to our usual lunch at the Picklonious Deli this year, with the stop at Taunton Bay Sweets afterward, and, of course, the back-to-school clothes-shopping trip at Renys. We always get that in before the crowds. And before all the plaid shirts are gone.

We're good at shopping. By that I mean we move

along so Frenchie doesn't get overwhelmed. A store like Renys can do that to him. Big space, bright lights. A lot of sounds, and people. What's new this year is that Cedar is fast on his feet. The second we wrestle our cart through the door he breaks away.

"Runner!" I cry.

Gracia is closest. She lunges and misses. Frenchie is gazing up at the ceiling lights. He's got his needlepoint purse tucked against his side like always. He's not much for running after Cedar anyway.

I am on it. Cedar's little sneakers slap along the tiled floor. I chase him through the shoe department, into the ladies' department. I run up behind him and almost knock him down. He points at a peg wall full of tote bags and pocketbooks.

"En-chee," he said. (That's what he calls Frenchie.)

"Yep, yep," I said. "Those purses are kind of like Frenchie's. But we don't need those today, Cedar Tree." I scoop him up. Lucky thing, he doesn't scream or twist— or worst of all, go limp. He can slide away like a hot stick of butter if he wants to.

I run him back to meet our cart in the boys' department. Gracia is holding a pair of khaki pants up to the backside of Frenchie, checking the fit. She gets him the same kind every year, except longer. Easy-peasy. Two pairs in the cart.

Mom hoists Cedar into the seat in the shopping cart.

41

"Let's hustle along," she sings, and Gracia laughs. All of us know, Cedar won't stay put for long.

"Next stop. Plaid shirts!" I say. (They *have* to be plaid.) I lead the way. Gracia makes a quick decision about size, then holds up three shirts in different plaids.

"Frenchie? Do you like these?" she asks. He doesn't answer, but he doesn't take the *no* pose either. In fact, he puts his arms around all three shirts and carries them to the cart. Sometimes, when he does stuff like that it makes Gracia cry.

As for me, I find things in the boys' and girls' departments. Today, it's three pairs of boys' sports shorts. Double mesh. Hems that hit below my knees, elastic waist with plenty of room, and my favorite thing, big deep pockets in front. I wear shorts all year, and leggings underneath when it's below freezing. But I'm not a kid who feels the cold much.

In the girls' department, I go round and round the racks, tapping every shirt on the shoulder with the palm of my hand. "Naw, naw, naw. Nope. Yuck."

"Take another look," Mom says.

"Eh. I got my old stuff. Still fits." (This argument is part of our back-to-school shopping tradition.)

"Understood," Mom says. "But your clothes have been worn hard, Aurora. It might be nice to have something without stains for picture day."

I groan. Then I spot a rack with tank tops on it. (They

can be impossible to find once fall comes.) "Yes!" I cheer. "Plain ones! No words or pictures!"

I grab up two, and Mom adds two more.

"Oh, and maybe . . . this!" I yank a zip-up hoodie off a circular rack. The hanger flips off the rack and flies over my shoulder. "Whoa!"

"Aurora. Go gently," Mom says, while Gracia hides a laugh.

"Can't help it!" I say. "They've got hoppin' hangers in here!" I bounce up and down and swing the hoodie in the air. Cedar is watching me. He starts to giggle.

Then I hear more giggling. I see two girls and two moms. One mom and daughter have dark tumbles of hair, almost exactly the same. They are wearing bright tunic tops with embroidery and mirror beads over their blue jeans. You could never find tops like that here in Renys. They look like something from India, I think. Then the mom speaks.

"How to put fun into a shopping trip!" Yep. I hear the Indian accent. Her dark eyes dance at Cedar. "That chuckle is so cute, don't you think so, Leena?" The girl grins and nods.

The other mom is redheaded, and the girl is very blond, with a pink sunburn on her nose, cheeks, and shoulders. Everyone is smiling, and I even see them notice Frenchie, who is being quiet beside our cart and staring up at the lights again. (Sometimes when there's a lot going on, Frenchie picks one thing to focus on.) The blond girl looks up like she's trying to see what he is looking at.

"It's the lights," I say. "Unless a bird got inside. Or a clothes hanger!" We laugh. I hold the hoodie up and make a goofy face. "Guess I'll try this on." I hope they'll stick around. I want to make them laugh some more. But they wave and disappear around the next aisle. Oh well.

Gracia, who Mom says is the best shopping partner ever, finds me two pairs of leggings.

"Love 'em!" I say. "Even better than the ones you picked for me last year."

"Oh good!" Gracia laughs. "It makes me cold to see your bare legs in winter."

"New can be nice. Besides, I did go through the knees of the old ones during mud season."

Mom stands by, nodding. I peel out of the hoodie, and Gracia hands me a long-sleeve tee. I slip it over my tank.

"It's *you*," Gracia says. I love that she knows what I like.

"It's me . . . as long as we can get this scratchy tag out of the neck. . . ." I reach back and tug at the neck of the shirt. I let out a growl.

"Of course," Gracia says. "We'll have our annual detagging ritual."

"Oh . . . meanwhile . . . you need underpants," Mom says, in her loud-mom voice.

"Oh, underpants, you say? Not sure the people over in the birdseed aisle heard you, Mom!" I point across the store, and Mom laughs. She takes Cedar, who wants out of the cart now anyway, to go find underpants.

Gracia and I look around some more, and Frenchie makes sure my clothes and his clothes have a nice space between them in the cart. He likes some things to be done a certain way. But something else seems to be bothering him. He's making little fists by his sides. I get an idea in my head.

"Hey, you want to push?" I say, and he steps right up.

He wraps his hands around the bar and starts the cart rolling.

"There ya go. Come on. We'll find my mom and Cedar. See if they've found me some *underpants!*"

"Aurora, you are a thoughtful friend," Gracia tells me as we stroll.

"Well, he asked for what he wanted," I say. "So, it's a little bit him asking and a little bit me guessing."

"Guessing correctly." Gracia uses her butter voice. "You are truly special."

I smile and give a little shrug, and think, I am Frenchie's special person. Then I remember the placement letters from the school. I swallow hard. Because the thing is, Frenchie is my special person too.

I think:

It's coming, Aurora. You're going to be in Ms. Beccia's class, but Frenchie will be in Mrs. Hillsbeck's. Apart.

I cannot picture it! My heart begins to sink.

Cedar comes running. His dark curls bounce on his head; his chubby cheeks bounce on his face. He's holding a pack of underpants by one corner, swinging it hard. He runs right at us and wriggles by.

I go after him, calling, "Cedar! Come back here with that!"

He stops and flings the package up in the air. It spins right up over the top of the display. I cover my mouth and catch Gracia's eye. We hear the package land in the next aisle over. Then a lot of laughing.

I race around the end aisle and see the two girls and two moms. Again! The sunburned girl is bent over laughing. The girl in the bright tunic smiles. She holds the pack of underpants out to me.

"I think these are for you?" I love how she says it and asks it all at the same time.

"Yup." I jab a thumb toward Cedar. "He tossed them. Up and over!" I say as Mom and Gracia and Frenchie meet us in the aisle.

Soon we are talking to Joanie Waller and her mom, from Collingswood, New Jersey, and Leena Virani and her mom, from Atlanta, Georgia. Ha! I think. The girl from away, and the girl from farther away.

The moms talk to each other, and the girls talk to me. Cedar climbs the side of the shopping cart, and Frenchie waits, but he faces away. Maybe he understands, or maybe he doesn't, but we are learning that both Joanie and Leena have moved to town. Both are new this year. And both will be in *my* sixth-grade class with Ms. Beccia.

"Beccia! Yes!" I whoop. I cover my mouth with both hands and bounce on the balls of my feet. I'm making Leena and Joanie laugh, and I love it.

The moms are agreeing that we should get together before the start of school—*and* that we should do that this Saturday at Pebble Nest. Leena and Joanie want to come! And me, I am thinking the strangest thing of all: it is possible that this is going well.

But then it starts. Frenchie sways and moans. There is too much going on inside of Renys now. Too much for Frenchie. These are new people. Everyone's excited, and we're talking too loudly, and all at once. He rocks and holds tight to the shopping cart. His moaning turns to a hollow woo-oo-woo-oo. All I can think is, we're going to have to leave, and I *so* don't want to.

I tell myself, Don't be *dirt*, Aurora.

I know Frenchie can't help this. He's in a super struggle. He's suffering. Gracia once said being upset gives him more pain than the times he's actually injured. We have to make it better for him. Right now.

Gracia is on it. She tells him, "I'm here. Frenchie." (The butter voice.) She takes a few steps with him. She turns to everyone and smiles her gentle smile. "We need

47

to move on toward the checkout. So, Rene, follow when-ever you're ready."

"We'll be right behind you," Mom says, and I know she means it.

"Right behind you," I echo. I feel pulled to go with them and pulled to stay where I am.

"Bye, Frenchie. Bye," Leena and Joanie and both their moms call after him softly. They seem to understand. Mom stays to get phone numbers.

"See you Saturday!" I tell the girls. I hustle to catch up to Gracia and Frenchie. She is cooing with him, letting him know she's there for him. She'll pull him out of this.

And she does. By the time we leave, Frenchie is more himself. He carries his new clothes in the Renys bag right against his chest. I'm more myself too. The Saturday plan with the new friends is a go! I am keeping a cork in my excitement. But I cannot fool Mom. She gives me a wink. She knows how I feel. I am over the moon!

In the evening, Frenchie and Gracia come to our house. Pop starts us a pancake supper. We like them fluffy, so he separates the eggs and whips the whites. Frenchie kneels on the kitchen stool and stares into the batter bowl. (He loves to watch the mixer.)

I hear Pop telling him, "See how it gets foamy first? Keep watching. Stiff peaks will form. . . ."

Gracia and Mom sit on the couch picking the stitches

out of the tags on some of the new clothes—mine and Frenchie's. We both go bonkers about tags. Sort of funny how the kid who likes his belt pulled tight can't stand tags. Me, I can't stand either.

I have built up some energy inside me tonight, and it wants out. I get on my back on the floor and do bicycle legs and fist pumps. I happened to look at Gracia as she leans down to bite a thread out of one of my new tops.

"Umm . . . pitooey!" she says. She picks the thread off her lip.

"Go, Gracia! Get 'em any way you can," Mom says with a laugh.

"Nice of you, doing all that thread picking," I say from my spot on the floor. I roll back and push up into a shoulder stand and continue to bike. "I don't have enough patience for that. Of course, if you know me, you know that."

"We're up to the challenge," Mom says. "I'm glad the back-to-school shopping is done." (She says that every year.) Mom mouths a thank-you to Gracia. She thinks I don't see her do it, but I do.

"Such a nice coincidence, meeting the new girls and new moms today," Gracia says. "I'm looking forward to Saturday."

"Umm," I say. But I hope she won't say much more about it. I let my shoulder stand go off-balance. Faking it.

"Whoa-whoa!" I grunt and pretend to concentrate.

I liked those girls, Leena and Joanie, and I felt like they already liked me back. Two new girls. In my class! Imagining what that would be like was getting all tangled up with knowing I wouldn't be with Frenchie.

How was he going do without me?

How would I do without him?

Aurora

The First Day of Sixth Grade

The last days of summer vacation are way different than any before. Joanie and Leena and their moms come to Pebble Nest. The Viranis surprise us all when they drive up in their shiny new food truck, with Leena's big sister, Zenia, on board. She is our server. We have Virani Family Indian Cuisine for lunch. I fall in love with potato-and-pea samosas with tamarind sauce.

I keep Frenchie in my sights—or I mean to. But I get busy sketching Leena and Joanie a map of the school. Everything will be new for them. When I look up, Frenchie is wading at the edge of the water and Gracia is sitting on the beach with Joanie's mom. Frenchie is on a break. A people break.

We keep all our end-of-summer dates with Frenchie and Gracia. He likes those days best, when he knows what to expect. But he and Gracia come for a lunch date at Joanie's house one day, and we all hike the Hidden Ponds Loop another. Frenchie is most comfortable staying off to the side, a bit ahead or behind. I am completely comfortable everywhere. I am having a ton of fun.

On the last weekend before school begins, we host a sixth graders' super-supper cookout at the A-frame. Gracia has us all making personal pizzas on the grill. Pop lights candle lanterns, and Mom builds us a campfire for toasting marshmallows and pineapple kebabs. We tell not-very-scary ghost stories.

And now I don't want summer to end.

It's a good thing school always starts just before Labor Day. Three days to get used to it. Three days off. Then a short week. It's like a break at the beginning.

The air still feels like summertime on our first day of sixth grade. I wait with Frenchie at our bus stop. I scuff up the gravel, pacing left, then right. I get the same old feelings. Fresh start coming. Helene will drive our bus again. The floor mats will smell clean and rubbery until someone spills milk or yogurt and sours them up.

For days I've been reminding Frenchie, "Mrs. Kingsley will meet us. Like always. And I'll walk with you to *your* classroom. But then I'll have to go down the hall to *mine*." He doesn't answer. Not in a way that anyone else would understand. But I see the little fist squeezes.

I lean toward him and whisper, "I know. I'm not so sure about this either."

He raises his shoulder up. "Oops. Sorry. Gave you an ear-tickler, didn't I?"

Then it turns out I am wrong. Mrs. Kingsley is not there—or at least she isn't there to meet us. I can see through the glass panel that the office is full of kids and parents with first-day-of-school problems to sort out. But I know where Frenchie's classroom is. (Our school is small.) We can get there on our own.

A guy meets us at the door. At first I think he's another kid. But then he speaks and his voice is deep. He's a man. He's young.

"Oh! Hello, you must be Frenchie," he says. Frenchie stares past him. Then the guy looks at me. "And you must be Aurora."

"Am," I say. "You already heard about me, huh?"

"I heard Frenchie would be coming in with you," he says. "I'm Mr. Menkis. I'm a very recent hire. I just got off the phone with Frenchie's mom. Mrs. Whilmer and I called to let her know I'm Frenchie's new aide."

I raise my eyebrows. "*You are?* Wonder what happened to Mrs. Kingsley," I say.

Mr. Menkis shrugs. "A last-minute change."

"Are you old enough to teach here?" I ask. "Because, um . . . you are small. I mean short."

"I am short. But yes, I can teach here. Today's my first day," he says.

"So you mean we're about to find out." I rock my head from side to side.

He sputters a little, and I think he's trying not to laugh.

I decide that Mr. Menkis is cheery but not in a drive-you-nuts way like some people are when they meet Frenchie. *Overly effusive* is what Mom and Gracia call that. It's when people are too loud and too happy, and talk fast. It makes me feel like they're afraid to leave any space between their words because if they do, something could go wrong in there. Frenchie and I both get some *overly effusive* greetings from adults when they first meet us. I shrug it off. But nothing makes Frenchie cross a room faster.

"We thought you'd be waiting out front," I tell Mr. Menkis. "That's how this usually works."

"Well, I was there. But your bus was delayed this morn—"

"Well, that happens a lot on the first day," I say. "Oh. Sorry for interrupting."

"Sure. The office was going to call me—"

"Oh. The office." I roll my eyes. "It's a circus in there. More first-day stuff."

"Right. Well, I came back down to steal a few minutes and set up Frenchie's desk. So thanks for escorting him,

Aurora. I've got it from here. You can go on to your class-room," he says. "The day is about to begin."

"Hmm. Well, I promised Frenchie I'd walk him *into* his room. He'll take that to heart," I say.

I point a finger and repeat, "*Into.*"

"That works for me," Mr. Menkis says, "at least for today." He steps aside.

Frenchie's classmates are sitting down, which means mine are too. Down the hall. His classroom teacher, old Mrs. Hillsbeck, is up in front getting ready to take atten-dance. I think she's been around since our school was built, and that was a long time ago. That's how it is in our town. Teachers either stay a really long time or a really short time.

I see Frenchie's name tag taped to the top of his new desk. There are three bird identification cards all in a row.

"Oh, hey. Great idea!" I say. I give Mr. Menkis a nod. "Frenchie is all about birds."

"This is what I hear."

"See his needlepoint purse? Get him to show you what's in there."

"I sure will," he says.

"Great . . ." I want to stay longer. Maybe until lunch-time. Maybe until the last bell.

"Okay, Aurora . . ." Mr. Menkis looks at his watch. I take the hint.

"Going," I say.

But first I tell Frenchie I'll see him at lunch and recess. I want him to be okay. My own armpits feel a little cold and sweaty as I go out that door.

Ms. Beccia is probably going to pronounce my last name wrong. My whole class is going to crack up.

"Can't wait." I sigh and roll my eyes on my way down the hall.

Then I remember that I'll have two new friends in my classroom. Joanie and Leena. The girl from away, and the girl from farther away.

"Yes!" I pull up on the straps of my backpack and go speed-walking down the hall.

Aurora

Preposterous Pursuits

The first morning of sixth grade flies by. Ms. Beccia is a funny, laugh-out-loud teacher! She gets my last name right! She lets Leena and Joanie and me push our desks together in a triangle. I don't have to worry about Darleen Dombroski because she is not in my class. She's down the hall with Mrs. Hillsbeck. And Frenchie. When I think about Frenchie, I want to run and peek inside that room. But Ms. Beccia's classroom is a busy place. We're doing math already. (Placeholders and rounding.) Since Frenchie and I were never in this room together, I'm not looking for him here the way I thought I'd be.

At lunchtime, I take hops ahead of Leena and Joanie. At the door to the multipurpose room, I point them to the small round table tucked up beside the stage. "Frenchie and I sit there, a little bit apart, because lunchtime gets noisy," I say. "But see? There's room for four."

They go in while I wait for Frenchie. He comes down the hall, taking long Frenchie strides, with Mr. Menkis beside him. I wave my arm overhead. "Hey, Frenchie! How was it? Did you have a good morning?"

Mr. Menkis answers for him with a nod.

"I'll meet you at the door after recess, Frenchie," he says. "Enjoy your lunch. You as well, Aurora."

"Thanks, Mr. Menkis! You too!" I turn to Frenchie. "Come on," I say. "Leena and Joanie are already at our table."

I make sure he gets the chair he is used to, the one that faces the stage. He twists it a hitch, so he is turned slightly away from us. He does that around the new friends, I have noticed. But he opens his lunch and begins to eat.

Leena opens a container of Indian food. In seconds, the air around our table smells unbearably fantastic. She digs into her backpack and brings out a notebook.

"Look," she says. Big smile. She flashes the cover. I see hand lettering.

Joanie reads. "'Preposterous Pursuits.'" She raises her eyebrows. "What's this?"

"Okay." Leena takes a breath like she's been dying to tell us. "I have been thinking about this since new students' orientation day. Preposterous Pursuits is a list

58

of activities to do during recess. The expected, *and* the unexpected. Think *challenges*," she says. "Think, *scavenger hunt*. The idea is, we put that playground to the test."

"You mean, explore its possibilities?" I ask.

"Exactly! And we work as a team. No winners or losers. Just things to do. All of us. Together."

"Wait. I need an example," Joanie says.

"Okay, sure." Leena opens the notebook. "So one of my ideas is the Acorn Carry. For this one, you pile as many acorns as you can onto *one* hand. Keep your other hand behind your back and walk from the oak tree back to the blacktop. The blacktop is our home base. The idea is to *collectively* bring as many acorns home as we can."

"Oh . . . I think I get it." Joanie nods.

I stay quiet because I'm thinking.

Leena reads more examples. "Dog and Bone. One person is the *dog* with a blindfold on, and they have to guess who snuck up and stole their bone. Human Sundial is the coolest. We'll need chalk for that one. High-Water Mark. We jump up and scratch a mark with a stone in the brick wall, as high as we can reach. And we can brainstorm more!" Leena holds her pencil ready.

I glance at Frenchie beside me. Still turned away and nibbling on his sandwich. I wonder how he'll do with Preposterous Pursuits. . . .

"Bird Search!" I blurt. "Oops. Sorry so loud."

"It's perfect!" Leena adds my idea to the list.

"Hundred-Yard Dash!" I lean toward Frenchie. "Every day, right? And we'll try the other pursuits too. Okay?"

He pulls his elbows in. Leena catches my eye.

"If anyone wants to opt out of a pursuit, that's totally fine," she says. "We can revisit any one of them any time."

"Ya know what?" Joanie tilts her head. "We should keep count. In the notebook. Add a tally mark for every hundred yards we run. For challenges like the Acorn Carry, we can try to best ourselves. We can keep a bar graph!"

Leena squeezes Joanie's arm. "Yes!"

"Record the results!" I clap my hands. "Genius! This whole thing is genius! And, Leena, you better give each challenge its own page."

"Oh. My. Gosh! Yes." She flips to a blank page and makes the first header: 100-YARD DASH.

Before we leave the lunch table for our first recess of the year, we have added half a dozen pursuits to Leena's list. When we get outside, we dive right in.

It goes okay. For Frenchie, I mean. He follows a few steps behind me for a round of Garbage Grab. That's Joanie's idea. We go around the edge of the playground picking up paper litter. (Nothing gooey.) We fill up the brown bag from her lunch in no time, and dump it in the receptacle.

"We need more bags!" I say. "Lot of litter!" We make Garbage Grab a Priority Pursuit. Leena stars the page.

Joanie writes the date and draws a picture graph: one bag.

I *love, love, love* the way this is coming together.

But Frenchie doesn't. He twists his fingers into the strap of the needlepoint purse and goes to pace at the edge of the blacktop.

I turn to Joanie and Leena. "It's time. Gotta dash," I say. "Hundred yards, that is." It splits me up from them. (They are not dashers.) I don't mind so much because Frenchie and I will earn two tally marks for the book.

I call to him. "Ready, set, go!"

By Friday, the third day of school, I am sure of three things: Preposterous Pursuits will be never ending. And never boring. *And* I have *friends*!

I run the second hundred-yard dash of the day with Frenchie. We've worn a pair of paths, from the edge of the blacktop to the backstop, and not because of Preposterous Pursuits. We started this way back. I do the math: 180 days of school each year (minus a few for bad weather), multiplied times three. Whoa! 540 days of running! We have wrecked the grass. We have left our mark.

We reach the backstop, tag it, and turn. Running back, I've got my eye on Leena and Joanie. They're on the blacktop together, notebook open. On the ground beside them is the yardstick Ms. Beccia let us borrow. We need it for measuring Hop, Skip, and Jump and High-Water Mark. We're trying to do both today because tomorrow is the start of a three-day weekend, and Leena likes setting goals.

Frenchie and I finish our run, and Joanie cheers, "The Hundred-Yard Dash page is filling fast!"

"Whew!" I lean over my knees and breathe. Frenchie switches to pacing. "Hear that, Frenchie? The tally is climbing. All because of you!"

Yesterday, we played Bird Search, with Frenchie in the lead, but I'm not sure he knew he was leading. We walked under the trees with him and counted all his flaps and tweets. Mrs. Woodsum came over to see what we were doing.

"Girls," she said, her eyebrows low, "this seems a bit unkind."

"What? Why?" I asked. Joanie and Leena stood beside me looking petrified.

"I see you writing in a notebook every time Frenchie flaps his hands." Mrs. Woodsum shakes her head. "And I hear a lot of giggling." She gives us a look. Stern and disappointed. "Girls, Frenchie's not able to control—"

"Wait. No," I said. "Sorry for interrupting. But it's *not* unkind. I get why you could think that, Mrs. Woodsum. But this is a game about spotting birds. Perfect for a kid who loves them."

"W-we're including him," Joanie whispered in a mouse voice.

Well, big surprise. Mrs. Woodsum accepted my explanation and left us to our bird search. Leena and Joanie thought I was brave for standing up to her.

"Well, I've had experience," I said. "If you mess up, admit it. But if you didn't, you should say so."

"Defend the truth!" Joanie said, her fist in the air. That made us laugh.

"Mrs. Woodsum should know better," I mumbled. "I've been Frenchie's friend for a long time."

"I bet she saw it differently because Joanie and I are here too," Leena said.

Things have been different, and nobody feels it more than Frenchie. I can see. He paces when I poke my nose into the Preposterous Pursuits notebook. He does hand squeezes if a pursuit takes too long. Then I have to stop and do another dash with him. A couple of times now, I've thought I should drop out of Preposterous Pursuits. But I like it too much to leave it.

Today, with two runs done, Leena and Joanie and I go on to Hop, Skip, and Jump. (I cannot get Frenchie to try, even when I remind him that birds hop too.) We take running starts and hop, skip, and jump. We use Ms. Beccia's yard stick to measure our distance. From the corner of my eye, I see Frenchie pacing.

"Hey," I say, "we already did two runs. Give me a few minutes, okay?"

It's not okay. I know it's not. But I feel a little burn. Frustration is what that is.

When Leena and Joanie gather up the notebook and the yard stick and head to the brick wall for High-Water Mark, I go. I'm in a jumping mood. I jump all the way to the wall, all of us laughing. Except Frenchie. I call for him to come. I wind my arm round and round. Joanie tries to get him. But he walks wide to avoid her.

Then I hear it. "Woo-woo . . ." and I stop in my tracks.

"Woo-woo . . ." At the edge of the blacktop, Frenchie sinks to the ground.

"Oh no . . ."

He tucks up like an egg.

"Frenchie! It's okay!" I go to him, but I'm too late.

He folds his arms over his head and shuts down.

I sit beside him while Joanie and Leena speak to the playground monitor. She sends them to get Mr. Menkis.

Aurora

Waiting on Frenchie

Mr. Menkis does exactly the right thing. He doesn't rush up. He arrives, and brings the calm with him. He sits down with Frenchie and me. He asks everyone to give us some space. Perfect word. This is Frenchie's space. Like Gracia told us years ago, it's the space he makes for himself when he needs it. Our job is to sit near and talk softly. That's what Mr. Menkis and I do.

The recess bell rings. I give Leena and Joanie the tiniest finger wave as they join the line to go inside because, of course, I'm staying with Frenchie.

"Any idea what happened?" Mr. Menkis asks.

"Yeah." I puff out a breath. "I've been doing stuff he isn't used to, and it messes with him." I explain about

Preposterous Pursuits and hundred-yard dashes. "The problem is, I need to be in two places at once," I say. "It's impossible."

"Ahh . . ." Mr. Menkis nods.

"I feel bad about it . . . but . . ." I shake my head and don't finish.

"You're having a new kind of year." Mr. Menkis says it for me. "Treat yourself sweetly, Aurora. Change happens. It's the world's number one constant." He pushes his feet out in front of him, and his hands behind him. He tilts his head back so his face is in the sun.

I do the same. I whisper, "S-s-sun sure feels good right now. Feel it, Frenchie?"

"Do I hear sparrows?" Mr. Menkis asks softly. He gives a low whistle, follows with a cheepity-cheep-cheep.

We are waiting for Frenchie to feel like himself again.

"Aurora," Mr. Menkis says, "keep in mind, having new friends doesn't mean you're leaving someone else behind."

"Thanks, Mr. Menkis. Nice of you to say it."

Beside me, Frenchie begins to relax. He lowers his arms. He stretches one leg forward.

"You're like a bird leaving the egg," I tell him. "You're hatching."

Ed Petrequin

In the Drop-Off Circle

Ed Petrequin arrived at Mountain View School's morning drop-off circle a little on the early side the first Friday in September. Cedar had a morning appointment with the ear doctor over in Ellsworth. Given the late-summer traffic, the sooner Ed got on the road, the better. Aurora and Frenchie both hopped out onto the sidewalk. In the back seat, Cedar cried out.

"Bye-baw! Bye-baw!"

His little boy had something to say. Ed was sure of it, and he was trying his darnedest to understand. But he had his eye on Aurora and Frenchie too. The boy was staring off, which he did quite often. Ed waited to make sure Aurora circled back to collect him. And she did. She turned him toward the front doors of the school. Ed felt proud. Aurora was a good human. Of course, he'd always known that. But this year, he'd seen her mature—and she'd done it in her own good time, by being exactly who she was.

"Love you, my girl. Love you," he whispered. Ed knew she was too far away to hear him. But he leaned and stretched his arm toward the passenger's side window, hoping Aurora would see him wave goodbye one last time. She and Frenchie merged with all the other kids—heads and backpacks—through the open door.

Cedar was upset now, arching his back and kicking his legs.

Doesn't like that car seat, Ed was thinking. Too confining for Cedar, who had skipped walking and gone right to running. Ed was an old father. He sighed a little when he thought about the hours ahead. Rene had a story to write, and she'd taken Gracia with her to Camden the previous afternoon at Ed's suggestion. A night away from home was a rare treat for both of them. Ed was in charge of the three kids. Aurora and Frenchie were easy. But Ed felt like he'd chased Cedar all evening long, and finally, into bed. Phew. Ed had collapsed on the couch, fallen asleep with his boots on.

Aurora had helped. She always did. Now she and Frenchie were in school. Ed was on his own. He'd be running after Cedar all day. The women wouldn't be back until after three o'clock.

"That's okay," Ed said, and he smiled. "They're getting a nice pampering." He was happy for both Rene and Gracia.

Ed was yawning, so he missed the moment when his little boy pointed his plump finger toward the side yard of the school.

"Bye-baw! Bye-baw!" Cedar cried, and he kicked.

"What is that about?" said Ed. He glanced into the back and saw Cedar put his finger into his ear.

Not another infection, Ed thought. Well, good time for a checkup.

"I'm so sorry, my boy. I don't understand . . ."

The toddler sat back in the car seat, gave a whimper of defeat. One last time, he whispered, "Bye-baw . . ."

Ed let the car idle forward. A few feet from the back bumper of the car in front of them, he gently pressed the brake again. Then again. "Well, little buddy. There's no use being anything but patient. The school circle is a traffic jam. That's why we like the school bus. How about we sing?" Ed said. "Want to sing?" He cleared his throat and found his old college choir baritone. "'I've been workin' on the railroad, all the live-long day. . . .'"

Cedar sang the next line along with his pop. "Yidee yidee yidee-YAY-yo . . . ahh-dah yah-yah-yah-yah YAY. . . ."

Frenchie

During Arrivals

Frenchie stood in the narrow side yard outside the school, looking back at the glass door. He could see himself in it. Tan pants and plaid shirt. Belt tight. On right. He watched himself pat the needlepoint purse at his side.

Frenchie waited to disappear. That would happen when Aurora swung the door to come out and go with him. The Frenchie in the glass would fold away, then come back again when the door closed. That was how the door with glass worked.

He waited.

Aurora didn't come.

He heard birds chattering in the skinny trees. Frenchie loved the way birds opened themselves. The wings. Turning colors off and on, flick quick, like his own blinking eye. He hugged the needlepoint purse. But he did not look up. He remembered something Aurora had once said:

You don't bother with birds at a time like this!

Aurora

Before Attendance

I'm leaning across the top of my school desk, belly and elbows. I'm holding half a split geode cupped in my hands. I'm keeping it out of sight for now. I've got a good story that goes with this old rock, and I'm dying to tell it to Joanie and Leena before attendance time.

"What do you have, Aurora? What's in your hands?" Leena's dark eyes shine.

"Yeah! Tell, tell!" says Joanie. She scoots her chair in to be closer.

"Well," I say, "have a look!" Slowly, I lift one hand away. All they see is a crusty brown rock in my palm.

"Oh . . . ," says Leena.

"What is it?" Joanie asks.

Very slowly, I turn the rock over and let them see the open side.

"Ooo! Crystals!" says Leena.

"Right!" I say.

"Like diamonds!" says Joanie. "Where did you get it, Aurora?"

"I'll tell you the story," I say. But that's as far as I get. Someone calls my name.

"Aurora?"

I slide back off the top of the desk and settle into my chair. I look around and wonder if it is someone who thinks they need to *speak* to me about climbing the furniture.

"Aurora." I hear it again. Then I see Mr. Menkis in our doorway.

"Oh, hey, Mr. Menkis." He takes a few steps into the room. I'm surprised to see him here.

"Aurora, did you see Frenchie this morning?" he asks.

"Yeah," I say.

"Did you come in together?"

"Yep."

"Okay," Mr. Menkis says. "Thank you."

He hurries out of the door.

"Huh. That was weird." I shrug at Leena and Joanie. "Bet Frenchie's looking out a window. Watching birds," I tell them.

"Probably," says Leena. She's seen how it is. How much he loves birds.

"Maybe he's in the bathroom," Joanie whispers.

"Yeah," I say. "Something like that."

Then our teacher, Mrs. Beccia, wants our attention. "Class, let's settle in and review today's schedule," she says. She turns to the whiteboard.

"Darn!" I say. There isn't time to tell the story of the geode.

Topher Menkis

Before Attendance

Topher Menkis knew when to expect Frenchie—*and* Aurora. The bus schedule had pretty well ironed itself out by the end of the second week of school. In respect for their friendship, and at the girl's suggestion, he'd been meeting the pair in the hallway, between the classroom door and the lobby. The distance was short. Administration had approved.

But this morning, Topher reached the ever-changing-tree mural in the school's front lobby without seeing either Frenchie or Aurora. He watched the stream of kids whose heads were, on average, about level with his own nose. He rose onto his toes, stretching upward for a better view of the bus circle.

Could he have already missed them?

Ah, there, he thought. He recognized the cluster of kids who were coming through the front door to the school. A back-of-the-bus bunch. This group was on his radar for two reasons. One, they rode Frenchie's bus. Two, he'd overheard one of them calling him Mini Menkis behind his back. Easy for Topher to shrug it off. No denying, he was probably the shortest school staff member these kids had ever met. He'd also been an elite college gymnast and knew the benefits of a low center of gravity.

So these were kids from the same bus . . . but something wasn't right. Frenchie and Aurora always sat up front. They should've entered the building well before this back-seat bunch—illustrious citizens of Mountain View School. Topher stepped into their path, stood tall and put up a hand.

"One second, please," he said, in his best Mr. Menkis voice. "Was Frenchie on the bus this morning? Or Aurora?"

The bunch shrugged in unison. Avoided eye contact.

But one voice answered. "We sit in the back. Never really see them. Probably gone down the hall already."

"Right," Topher said. "Onward, then. Thank you. Have a good day, people."

He thought to dash out and ask the bus driver, but it was too late. She had already pulled on through the loop.

Before he went in search, he leaned around the glass

partition to speak to the school secretary. "We don't have a sick call on Frenchie Livernois this morning, do we?"

"On Frenchie?" The secretary scrunched her brow. She checked all the Post-it squares on her desk, then her computer screen. She shook her head. "No . . . nothing . . ."

"Okay. Didn't really think so. I'm supposed to receive a message if he's going to be absent, and I don't have one. I must have missed him," he said, keeping his voice even. But in truth, Topher Menkis was mystified, and a little worried as he hustled on down the hall. Frenchie had had a terrific second week—and only the one upset on the playground last week. But Topher's concern grew when he didn't find Frenchie in his classroom.

There had to be an explanation. . . .

Aurora.

He hurried down the hall and peeked into her classroom. There she was! At her desk—*on it*, actually—belly surfing, and talking to the two new girls. She had her feet hooked into the back of her chair, and it bobbed as if she were towing it behind her.

But no Frenchie.

He stayed only long enough for her to tell him that yes, Frenchie was at school today. He double-timed it into the boys' bathroom to see if Frenchie had made a stop, then back to his classroom for one last look. Empty desk.

Topher took no chances. He dialed the school office from the hall, as he turned in full circles, looking up and down the corridor still hoping to spot the boy. The secretary answered. Topher informed her that they may have a problem. He did not have eyes on Frenchie Livernois. "Please inform Principal Whilmer—*right away!*"

Less than three seconds later, Topher heard the weirdly pleasant-sounding *bong-bong* of the outer door alarms. In the now-quiet hall, he listened to the automatic dead-bolt locks slide and click into place on all the doors at Mountain View School.

Lockdown.

Aurora

As Class Begins

Ms. Beccia is still going over our schedule for the day when we hear a sound—a sort of *bong-bong*. It is coming from the hall. Every head turns toward the door. We ask, "What is that?" Did somebody lean on a button they shouldn't have? Ms. Beccia takes a call on the classroom intercom.

Next thing I know, our school principal, Mrs. Whilmer, and her assistant, Mrs. Delano, come into our classroom. They stoop beside my chair. We are eye to eye.

Am I in trouble?

In a whispery voice, Mrs. Whilmer says, "Excuse me. Aurora, we're looking for Frenchie. Did you see him this morning?"

"Oh yeah, I already told Mr. Menkis. He's here. Frenchie's here."

Mrs. Whilmer does not look convinced. "Wait," I say, "are you telling me Mr. Menkis didn't find him? Sheeshy-sheesh!" I rock my head from side to side.

"Sometimes he wanders a little. You know," I say, because Mrs. Whilmer has known Frenchie for three years, same as I have. "He never goes far." I push up out of my chair. "I'll help you look."

"Thank you, Aurora." Mrs. Whilmer stands and puts a soft hand on my shoulder, but it *is* a stop-you hand. "We will want your help in a few minutes. We have a procedure to follow, so it's important for all students to stay in their classrooms for now. But I will come get you as soon as the situation allows." Mrs. Whilmer and Mrs. Delano head for the door.

Situation?

"Well, okay," I call after them, "but I could be helping yoooouu . . ." I hold the note.

I sit back down. Joanie and Leena look at me with big round eyes. I flap a hand.

"He'll turn up," I say. "But why can't I go look for him? Why don't we all look for him?"

Aurora

Frenchie's Way of Whistling

I know my friend. If he's not in this school building, then he's outside looking up into the trees, searching for birds. I see him do it all the time. We go hiking and he will stop still, all of a sudden. I freeze in place too, and I whisper in the lowest whisper I can, "Bird?"

Frenchie answers by keeping his body still. He stares, more than he watches. I am never sure at what. I face the same way he faces. I scan all around us. Most of the time, I'll find the bird. We both stay still until it leaves. Then he flaps his hands and lets out a whistle. He doesn't smile. But I know that's Frenchie being happy.

Pop says Frenchie's whistle is musical. I'd say that's right. Little bit tweety, little bit twittery. He uses his lips to make a little hole to blow through. He does something with his tongue inside his mouth that breaks the sounds into short bursts. Pop said that's called staccato. Gracia told us Frenchie did that on his own; she never taught him. I believe her, because even though we got Frenchie to float, and even swim, it can be hard to teach him things.

Gracia said Frenchie never played with toys. But by the time he was three, he was all about birds. "There's no telling why." She said it with a soft smile. "He'd watch them at our feeder, and everywhere we went. He started to flap his hands like little wings, and raise his chin and purse his lips, like making a beak." Gracia laughed. "One day, he whistled!"

That pretty whistle is one of the only sounds that Frenchie Livernois makes, and it is like birdsong. But it isn't exactly like any of the bird calls I know. I thought about it once: birds have beaks, not lips, and I think they make sounds in their throats. Quite a bit different from Frenchie's tweet. He doesn't pipe like the Carolina wren, doesn't coo like a mourning dove. He doesn't make the cheepy-chatty sound of a finch, and he doesn't buzz like a chickadee. And thank heavens he doesn't scream like a blue jay.

If I had to pick, I'd say his song is closest to the oriole. Come to think of it, that's probably why the oriole call is my favorite.

Aurora

Anybody Here Seen Frenchie?

Mrs. Whilmer and Mrs. Delano are back again. Our security guard, Mr. Gessup, is with them.

"Quiet, please. May we have your attention?" Mrs. Delano speaks.

Then Mrs. Whilmer raises her hand and asks, "Has anybody here seen Frenchie Livernois this morning?"

Leena, Joanie, and I raise our hands. But every set of eyes is on me. People know that he's always with me. Has been for the last three years.

"You still haven't found him?" I say, waving my hand over my head.

"We have not," Mrs. Whilmer says. She asks each of us where we saw him.

"Coming in this morning," says Joanie. "At the front doors."

"Same," I say.

"And it was just for a quick second," Leena adds.

"Okay. Thank you, girls. Mr. Gessup has some thoughts for all of us," she says. "This is very important. Please be good listeners."

Mr. Gessup holds up Frenchie's school portrait. He smiles. "I think all of you already know what Frenchie looks like."

"But that's from last year," I say. "He has longer hair right now." I put a finger in the air and add, "Sorry for interrupting."

Mr. Gessup says, "That's okay. Details are important. For instance, Frenchie wears tan pants and plaid shirts, and he carries a big shoulder-type bag—"

"It is a needlepoint purse! He keeps bird pictures in it. Another detail," I say.

"Thank you, Aurora. So, we'd like everyone to think very hard about what you saw this morning. Retrace your path in your mind's eye. If you walked to school, did you see anything unusual? If you rode your bus, did you see Frenchie? Was he in the drop-off circle? Or somewhere else around the building?"

I shake my head. Frenchie doesn't do that.

"If you think of something—anything—even if it

doesn't seem important to you, we'd like to hear about it. Just ask your classroom teacher for permission. Feel free to talk to us." He sweeps his arm in a friendly way. Mr. Gessup is being chirpy this morning. It's a little weird.

"Nobody is in trouble," he says. "Nobody is *going* to get in trouble. We expect Frenchie will be found safe and sound, probably before lunchtime." He rubs his belly, like he's already hungry.

There are some laughs. Tiny ones.

"That's right," Mrs. Whilmer says. "We are a community, and we all want to find Frenchie. So do that little bit of work with us and use your memories. Think about this morning," she says, "and, please, if you have ideas, if you know things Frenchie likes to do, something you have seen him take an interest in, let us know. Our police and the security guards from our other schools are arriving to help us look."

The police?

"You'll see them outside the windows and in our hallways. They may pop into your room. Thank you all very much." She adds a soft smile. She and Mr. Gessup stand together near the door. They talk in low voices.

"Aurora," Leena whispers. "Are you all right?"

"Well, I think I am. But that part about the police? Sheesh."

"I know. . . ." Joanie scrunches her brow. Other kids

are looking at me. I think everyone expects me to be bonkers right now. Should I be?

I lean across the desks to get closer to Joanie and Leena. "Frenchie doesn't get lost," I say. "The more you get to know him, the more you'll see it. We hike all over the woods, bird-watching, and rock hunting, and Frenchie makes it home *before me* most of the time. He gets me unlost. Like a human compass."

Joanie nods. "He was the first one back to the trailhead the day we hiked Hidden Ponds Loop," she says.

"He always knows the way," I say.

I think how this past weekend Frenchie and I were out for hours in one of our favorite places, Sundrop Meadow. Right behind our houses. On the way home, I kept picking up rocks and stopping to throw them. Soon, Frenchie was out of sight. I don't worry when that happens. But I hustle a little to catch up. We crossed the blueberry fields, then I saw his plaid shirt and the reddish square of the needlepoint purse disappearing into the pines up ahead. I stopped at his house to make sure he was there. I wasn't even up the steps when Gracia called from the kitchen window, "He's here! Thanks, Aurora."

"Aurora?" Mrs. Whilmer is speaking to me. "Will you come now?" she says. "We could really use your help."

I'm on my feet. I follow the adults into the hall. Weird look to the place. Every classroom door is closed. Mrs. Whilmer says she's going to check in with staff members who are looking for Frenchie inside the building, then meet the police officers. So I'm with Mr. Gessup.

"Come on, my friend," he says. "Let's go outside and see if we can find the boy with the needlepoint purse."

Aurora

The Day Frenchie Got the Needlepoint Purse

I walk the playground ahead of Mr. Gessup. I look through the tree trunks, beyond the fence, and make chirping, cheeping sounds. A few police officers are picking through the woods. Seeing them puts a pit in my middle.

Across the schoolyard our custodian opens the utility shed. (They're searching everywhere.) Mr. Menkis is there too. He vaults onto the lid of the dumpster, then up to the shed roof, graceful as a cat. Wow! He stands at the roof ridge and scans the grounds.

I try to spot a patch of plaid in the woods, or a dash of red. The needlepoint purse.

I was with Frenchie the day he got that purse. Hot, horsefly kind of day in late July. It was the summer before we started fourth grade. I'm sure, because I know we didn't have Cedar. Not quite yet.

Gracia took us to our favorite Route 1 flea market at Baker's Field. She said for fun, but I knew it was because Mom and Pop wanted me out of their hair while they were painting our kitchen floor. (I can be quick and forgetful, and I step in things like wet paint.) Frenchie will always go to a flea market. There's no better place to find bird pictures on the cheap.

I watched his face as we bumped along looking for a parking spot in the shade. It was the chin-up face. That's a ready face. He loves scouting for bird pictures, and when he gets to the kind of place he can do that, he knows it. You won't see Frenchie jumping up and down about that—or anything else, really. But if you watch—if you really *see* him—his face will say it all: *I've got business here.*

There was a big summer crowd that day. We'd been there all of fifteen minutes when Frenchie stalled out at Mrs. Thrift's camper van. She's a regular. Her spot always looks like she opened her camper door and shook all the stuff out of it. Then she spends the day sorting everything onto blankets. From what I've seen, she finishes just about in time to pack it all up again. Her husband always helps her. She tells him what to do.

I'm thinking Mrs. Thrift is not her real name. But that's what it says on the pin she wears on her front. The pin is as big as a tea saucer with a lace ruffle around the edges. Cumbersome is how that looks. But the black letters on the yellow background do catch your eye. She always hangs a matching sign off the sideview mirror of her camper van. Good advertising.

Anyway, Frenchie picked up the wide, flat needlepoint purse. The stitches made a pattern of fall leaves, nuts, and pine cones in red colors mostly, with some dark green and brownish gold. It had a long shoulder strap on it with a brass buckle, and a zipper across the top to keep it closed. He worked his hands all along the edges of the bag.

"So, ya like it?" I asked. I leaned in and gave the bag a sniff. Kind of musty. I rubbed my nose. Slapped a green-headed fly off my arm. Boy, were we sweating.

"I like it too," I told him. "Useful-looking, I'd say. Take it hiking, carry a water bottle, school papers . . ."

Mrs. Thrift kept her eye on us while she dusted a blue glass water pitcher. (I wondered how that got to the flea market in one piece.)

"He does like it," I told her. "I can tell."

Frenchie went to stand in front of Gracia. He rocked on his feet with the purse all scrunched up tight against his chest, and the price tag dangling out below his elbow.

"What do we have here?" Gracia caught the tag in her hand and took a look. She sighed. She looked at Frenchie. Then at Mrs. Thrift. "We'll take it."

"He wants the purse, does he?" Mrs. Thrift set the vase on a blanket and stuck her chin toward us.

Gracia held out a ten-dollar bill. "Yes, please."

"You're sure? I don't do returns," Mrs. Thrift warned. "What do you think he wants with a needlepoint purse?"

"I don't know." Gracia grinned. "But he doesn't ask for much. So . . ." She waggled the bill.

Mrs. Thrift narrowed her eyes and nodded. She trapped her giant Mrs. Thrift pin under her chin as she dug into her belt pack. She pulled out a five-dollar bill. "Half price. Today only," she said. She took Gracia's ten and gave her back the five.

"Oh, hey! That's a deal! You're a good old one, Mrs. Thrift!" I said. I punched my fist in the air. I spun on one foot.

"Very kind of you to do this for my son," said Gracia. (She always says *my son*.) "Thank you."

Frenchie was already heading back to the car with his new old purse. He knew what he wanted it for. A place to keep his bird pictures.

Aurora

Last Year When Frenchie Found the Nuthatch

I've got a joke I tell to Frenchie: "If I am a rock hound, does that make you a . . . bird hound?" I don't think he gets it. But I swear he would agree with me that the point is not to find everything at once. You love the hunt, and if possible, you don't take all the treasure when you do find it. Also, no getting disappointed if it takes a while to find the thing you want. Like me with the tourmaline; *that* is taking forever. So I love helping Frenchie find his birds. I end up being as much a bird hound as a rock hound. Last October, we went to Blue Hill to catch the last farmers' market of the season. We walked around eating empanadas, then went into town for ice cream, and I spotted the shop.

"Hold everything," I said, arms wide. "We have got to go inside."

"Clean hands first," Mom said. She handed Frenchie and me wet wipes.

The place was called Troviosity. The sign hung on a chain by the door. Mom said it sounded like someone had put the words *trove* and *curiosity* together. I knew what *curiosity* meant, because I've always been full of that. But Mom had to tell me that a trove was a collection of things, valuable or delightful.

"Well, matter of opinion, then," I said.

Our moms had a few more bites of their ice cream cones to go, and Cedar was still working on his kiddie serving. They stayed outside, on a bench in the sun, while Frenchie and I rushed up the steps together.

I gave the Troviosity sign a poke to make it swing. (Had to.) I was pretty sure Frenchie and I were thinking the same thing as I let us in the door: this was the kind of shop that might have bird prints.

Inside, there was a lot of flea market stuff—colored bottles and old silver coffeepots—mismatched forks and spoons. But everything was shined up and set out on fancy little tables and shelves. The shop smelled like cinnamon instead of dust and hot grass.

"Yeah," I said to Frenchie, "there could be birds for you here. Could be."

We started our search. The shop woman watched us through her skinny-rim glasses. She looked young, like a college student, and had warm brown skin and super-close-cut hair. She was smiling one of those worry smiles.

"Hi," I said. "I'm Aurora. This is Frenchie. He doesn't talk. We are both eleven. We don't break stuff."

"Oh, I'm sure you are fine." She threaded one finger through her dangly earring. "Looking for anything in particular?" she asked.

"Birds," I said. "John Audubon prints. Not framed. And since you said 'in particular'—a nuthatch. At least that's what I'm guessing."

I didn't explain because that could be too much talking. But the reason I was thinking nuthatch was because Frenchie had been watching one the morning before. Funny little thing that went traveling round and round the trunk of an oak tree. I say funny because a lot of the time, it was upside down.

"Well, all our unframed prints are here," the shop woman said. She showed me a wooden V-shaped rack. "You're welcome to look through. There was a set of Audubons, if I am not mistaken. Take a look."

"Okay, thanks. And hey, if you want to know, we did just have ice cream cones but we both cleaned up with wet wipes." I flexed my fingers for her. "Our moms will be in a minute with my little brother. He'll be cleaned up too."

"Perfection!" She smiled the better kind of smile. Her

phone buzzed over on the glass countertop above a jewelry case. "Excuse me, just a second," she said. "Feel free to interrupt me if you need to."

I called to Frenchie. "Hey. Over here. Could be the jackpot," I said.

I started to flip through the prints. All of them were wrapped in plastic. Maybe sticky ice cream fingers would not have mattered. "Let's see . . . boat, fish, boat, another boat, lighthouse, another lighthouse . . . third lighthouse . . . sheeshy-sheesh . . . lobster traps, fisherman, rocks, farmhouse . . . ah, *bird*." (I think it was a pelican.)

I paused, but Frenchie stared at that bird print like it was nothing but another lighthouse.

"Okay, okay. Not what you're after. Guess I knew that." I went on flipping prints. I got to a pack of pictures tied to together with a velvet ribbon. I pulled the bundle out of the rack. A sticker on the plastic sleeve said *Audubon/set* in pale pencil. I could see that the one on top was cardinals.

"You already have this same exact one," I said. I gave it a tap.

Frenchie did the slow blink.

"Yo, excuse me. Ms. Troviosity? Mind if I untie these?"

"Sorry?" She looked up from her phone. I pointed at the ribbon, then whirled my hand around. "Oh, sure. Go right ahead. And by the way, I'm Sheree." She pointed to herself and gave me a wink.

I gave her a thumbs-up.

"Let's see what's in here, Frenchie." I opened the pack and started to fan out the pictures.

There were six in all, and before I even got a good look, Frenchie had one in his hands.

"Oh! The nuthatch!" I blurted. "I knew it!"

Sheree came right over. (She probably wasn't used to loudness in the shop.) Frenchie clasped the print to his chest.

"You have just what he wants!" I said. "Unbelievable!"

"Oh, you found the Audubon set! So it's for him, is it? He likes birds?"

"He is all about them. How much? How much for that one? It's the nuthatch in case you wondered."

"The one? Oh, it's a set." She put her finger on her upper lip and frowned.

"Oh . . . ," I said. "Poo." I looked at Frenchie holding the print. I wanted him to have it. "Well, how much for the set, then?" I scrunched up my nose.

"Let me see, I thought there was a tag attached to the ribbon. Oh, here. Must have fallen." She bent to pick it off the floor.

"Sorry," I told her. "That's probably me who dropped it."

"That's okay. . . . Let me see. . . . Oh, Sixty-two fifty."

"Sixty-two *dollars* and fifty cents? That's expensive!" I said. I wiped my mouth with the back of my hand. "Sorry.

Little bit of spit there."

Sheree shrugged, as if she didn't mind the spit.

"Eh," I said, "his mom probably isn't going to go for that. I get that it's a great set of birds. And you wrapped them nice with the ribbon, and all. But there's a bird budget," I said. "Slim chance of a sale here."

"Oh, I see," she said. She looked sorry. She whispered to me, "I—I hope he's . . . not going to get upset if his mother says no."

"Naw. He'll just leave. Right out your door. Don't get me wrong, he'll still *want* the print. But he won't throw a tantrum, and he won't tear up your shop."

"I'm so glad. I don't want to hurt his feelings." She tilted her head and looked Frenchie over, probably no more than a second, but it seemed longer.

When Mom and Gracia came into the shop, there was a short discussion about the nuthatch being part of a set. Gracia gently took the print from Frenchie. She told him, in her usual quiet way, that the set was too expensive. "We'll find you the nuthatch. Some other time."

On our way out, I called over my shoulder, "See that? He's okay!"

The young woman nodded and smiled as she wrapped the velvet ribbon back around the set of prints.

We tried to stop at a bookstore right after that. I say tried because we had to leave pretty quick. Cedar was going to town, wiping out the picture-book shelves with a few quick swipes. So before you knew it, we were on the sidewalk again, heading for the parking lot.

"Oh, there you are! Wait!" We heard someone calling, but we all ignored it until we heard the same voice call louder and say, "Frenchie? It's Frenchie, right?"

That was weird because in all the time I've spent with Frenchie Livernois, I have never seen anyone running toward him calling his name. But Sheree from Troviosity was doing that exact thing. Her flat shoes smacked along the sidewalk. She waved a skinny paper bag in the air. When she reached us, she stopped to catch her breath. "Whew! The set . . . It doesn't matter. Who cares if it's five instead of six? Five is still a set, isn't it?"

"Oh my goodness," Gracia said. She put her hand on her chest, which is a very Gracia thing to do. "Thank you, but I think it is still probably too expensive for us."

"No, no. I want him to have it. Please. Here, Frenchie. Here's your nuthatch."

Frenchie stared straight ahead, never looked at her. It's not his way. But he put his hand right up, and she slipped that package into it. He blinked. She smiled, then watched as he slid the bag into his needlepoint purse. Then he started walking again.

We said thank-you for him. "That's not going to go to waste," I told her. "It'll be with him all the time. Every day." Mom and Gracia agreed with me.

"Nice of you, Sheree! You are the Nuthatch Lady!" I turned and called back to her. I even pointed both my pointer fingers at her and said it again. "Nice! Of! You!"

Then I added, "Thanks for *seeing* him!"

Maxine Grindel

Mrs. Thrift's Engine Trouble

If Maxine Grindel hadn't had her head under the engine hood of the old Mrs. Thrift camper van, she might have heard the gentle clacking of four cloven hoofs stepping across the road. She might have seen that most unusual-looking deer just before it became part of the weave of the blond-and-brown field at the side of the house. She might have noticed the way the late summer grasses closed, curtain-like, behind the deer's flicking tail.

Maxine was experiencing the great gift of determination that morning. The squealing of the camper van's aging fan belt had become unbearable on last week's trip to the Baker's Field flea market. If there was one thing Maxine knew about keeping an old engine healthy, it was that she better keep the one part that drives everything else shipshape. It wasn't an easy repair, but she'd done it before. Years ago. Maxine was good with her hands. With her two strong thumbs and few good grunts, she worked the new belt onto the pulleys and finally into place with a pop. There it is! Maxine thought. Mrs. Thrift will ride again!

The only help she had that morning was her husband, Dudley. All she needed him for was to start the engine on her command so she could see the new belt spin. Tricky business this was, because with the hood up Maxine and Dudley couldn't see each other.

"How about now?" Dudley barked out the driver's side window—for about the fifth time. He took a sip of his coffee, spilled some down his front, and flipped a page of the morning paper, which he had opened across the steering wheel.

Maxine straightened up and banged the top of her head on the hood latch. "Ow! Who put that there?" She rubbed her head with her palm and cussed a little. She barked back at her assistant, "Not yet!"

"All set? Did ya say?"

"Not now!" Maxine squawked. Dudley never listened! "I haven't even gotten the pulley adjusted . . . ," Maxine mumbled to herself.

While Maxine mumbled, Dudley said, "Gotcha, darlin'."

And while she tapped two fingers on the belt to check the tension, Dudley stretched his foot out and pressed the clutch to the floor. He turned the key in the ignition.

The engine turned over beautifully. The belt spun swiftly—and when it did, it sliced the tip of Maxine's right ring finger clean off.

Maxine might have screamed. For sure, she staggered back from the open hood. She held her finger tightly in her opposite hand and stared at it. She felt sealed in— as if a bubble had enclosed her, and for a few seconds, there was nothing except that whitish-pink place on her finger. Maxine made her eyes large and round. That was *not* the bone, she was pretty sure. Then Maxine had the dizzying thought that somewhere around her in the pine needles—or perhaps stuck to the hood or the engine of the camper van—was a piece of fingertip. . . .

About one-third the size of a cannellini bean, she thought.

And it was *her* fingertip. . . .

That she was not likely to find . . .

Ever.

Maxine felt cold. Her knees weakened. Blood came up in the end of her finger and poured down the sides like a candle spilling wax. Maxine stumbled. She saw Dudley coming around the camper for a look. She blinked. The world was disappearing now, and Dudley was going with it. Maxine was falling backward toward the ancient lawn chair beneath the broad pine.

If Maxine hadn't been blacking out, and if Dudley hadn't been running toward her, spilling coffee down his arm the whole way, one of them might have seen the boy in the plaid shirt come striding across Bert Gray Road and into the meadow at the side of the yard. And if Maxine hadn't been sinking through the weather-beaten webbing of the old lawn chair, she might have seen that strange, beautiful, unspeaking boy. She might have recognized him *and* the needlepoint purse he was clutching. Maxine Grindel—Mrs. Thrift—never forgot a sale.

Aurora

Thinking Back to Morning

We circle the school. No Frenchie. Mr. Gessup and I come to the tiny side yard. It's a narrow little nowhere spot at one end of the building. The kind of place nobody ever has a reason to be. There's a little ridge with a row of saplings. Mr. Gessup and I go up, calling Frenchie's name. I wait and listen, hoping I'll hear a rustle. Or, better, Frenchie's tweeting. But there is nothing.

I do what Mrs. Whilmer and Mr. Gessup wanted us to do. I hit the replay button in my brain. I think back over the morning from the time we got to school.

When we pulled into the drop-off, Cedar was bouncing up and down in his car seat and trying like the dickens to tell us something.

"Bye-baw! Bye-baw!" He kicked his feet out in front of him.

I told him, "Sorry, Cedar Tree. I don't understand."

Neither did Pop, and if Frenchie did, well, he wouldn't be able to tell us. Besides, he was staring out the car window and—

My own thought stops me.

I get that feeling—like I've been dunked in ice water. I turn to face Mr. Gessup.

"I was wrong!"

Mr. Gessup's eyes are round. "About what? What's the matter, Aurora?"

"I forgot!" I tell him. I turn and run down to the side yard door. I see my reflection in the glass. I look wild. I tug hard on the door. Then push it even harder. It doesn't budge. Then I remember: *lockdown*.

"Mr. Gessup!" I call. "Hurry! You have to get me in!" He comes running with his keys. "I forgot! We didn't even take the bus this morning!" I tell him. "Everything was different. I've *got* to tell Mrs. Whilmer! Right away!"

Aurora

Why Pop Drove Us to School in the First Place

I get to Mrs. Whilmer's office and it's like she knew I was coming. She catches me by my shoulders.

"We didn't take the bus! I completely forgot!"

"I know. It's okay, it's okay," she says.

"What do you mean okay? Did you find him?"

"Well, no, not yet. But I talked to your bus driver, Helene, and she told us you and Frenchie weren't on the bus this morning."

"Oh yes, Helene," I say. My heart is pounding.

"I called Frenchie's mom, and when we couldn't reach her, we called your dad, and he told us—"

"They are together!" I can't help interrupting. I'm bursting to explain the whole thing, and Mrs. Whilmer lets me. "My mom and Gracia are together. See, my mom had a story to write, about a new spa that opened at the Seacliffe Inn over in Camden. They have this thing called a Himalayan salt therapy room. Ugh. Not important," I say. "The place gave Mom a one-night stay for two."

"Got it," says Mrs. Whilmer. She's been nodding and listening. Being super nice.

I'm remembering how Mom had hesitated to go. She wanted to do the story but she didn't really care about spending the night or having the total spa experience. But the minute Pop heard about it, he'd said that Mom should go and take Gracia.

"Have a nice dinner in town," he said. "Sleep late. Get massages. Eat kiwis and chocolates." He said Frenchie could stay with us. And I said I'd help with Cedar. We wanted them to go.

So they did. They left yesterday afternoon, with little overnight bags, and they giggled like Leena and Joanie and Cedar and I would if we were going out for ice cream. I liked thinking of Mom and Gracia having that much fun.

I look at Mrs. Whilmer. "So Frenchie's mom went with my mom, and he stayed at our house last night. That usually doesn't happen. When you and Mr. Menkis asked me if Frenchie was on the bus, my brain was thinking about *usually*. Today was different. I'm really sorry, Mrs. Whilmer. Frenchie came to school with me. *In our car*."

"I understand how you forgot," she says.

"Pop brought us early because Cedar had a doctor's appointment in Ellsworth. He dropped us off. Right out front." I think for a second. "We met Leena and Joanie. We all came in together."

"Your dad says he saw Frenchie enter the building, just like you said." Mrs. Whilmer nods.

"I am one hundred percent sure," I say.

I have a little memory movie of that in my head. I see Leena . . . and Joanie. Trouble is, I can't see Frenchie.

I tell Mrs. Whilmer, "Frenchie was behind me. Indoors. But, I'm not sure if"—I take a swallow—"I don't remember stopping at his classroom door. Not today."

Aurora

The Ever-Changing Tree

I sit in the school office waiting for my parents and Gracia to pick me up. It's going to be a while. Pop will get home first but he'll have to wait for Mom and Gracia. They have a longer drive back to town. I keep leaning out to check the front doors. Mrs. Whilmer keeps promising me they are on their way.

This orange plastic chair is putting static electricity into my shirt. I can't sit still and I keep getting snapped. My hair is doing that thing where it flattens onto my face. Clinging. Like scared hair.

I see our art teacher, Ms. Chandra, through the glass. She's leading a small group of students. They're carrying neon-colored Post-its on their thumbs. They filter past

Ms. Chandra, then stop in front of the ever-changing-tree mural in the school lobby. It's a big bulletin board with a bare tree painted on it. Spreading branches. Like a yard maple. But that's not the point. Ever-changing. That's the point.

The winter I was in second grade, before I knew Frenchie, my class decorated the tree with snowflakes. Then we put up snow poems. I still remember mine:

Here comes the milk-white snow
I don't know the reason why.
Let's scoop it in our hands
And throw it back into the sky.

Then, last April, the third graders made pictures of bird's nests with eggs inside and put identification cards up to go with them. Frenchie and I stopped every morning to look at them. When school let out in June, there were illustrated folktales. For the start of school this year, there's a sign that reads: "Welcome, New Birds." Our seven new students, including Leena and Joanie, each have a colorful bird with their name and grade on it tacked to a high branch.

But the every-changing-tree is also a community board for all of us. We post news—everything from new kittens to losing a tooth. Birthday wishes and funny riddles. Even ice hockey scores. Darleen Dombroski once posted a note asking for help finding the heart-shaped locket she lost. (She got it back. She stopped crying.)

I watch the kids at the mural. They're sticking the bright Post-its onto the tree trunk. Ms. Chandra is close to me. I lean out of the doorway. "Hey, Ms. Chandra? What's going on there?"

"Oh, Aurora." Her dark eyes shine. "Some of my morning students felt distracted when they got to the art room. Everyone's thinking about Frenchie. They asked if they could write messages to him and post them on the tree."

"Messages, huh?"

"Yes. Good thoughts. Frenchie will see them when he returns." She dips her chin and smiles. "Meanwhile, we're sending positive energy to him." She hands me a Post-it and a marker.

"Positive energy. Like reaching him through the air?" I ask. Mrs. Chandra gives me a nod. But I am not sure that's possible. What's the energy source? Who or what steers the messages in the right direction—and if something out there knows which way to go to find Frenchie, why doesn't it give us a clue? Or better still, tell us where he is? Then I think this: If Frenchie is here, like hiding here in the school, I'm going to be mad. Because this is really starting to hurt. I curl back into the plastic chair in the office to wait.

111

Aurora

The Poem Barn

I have sat in this school office plenty of times. Usually because I'm in some sort of trouble and I am waiting to hear what Mrs. Whilmer has to say about it. Today, that stuff feels like nothing. I drop my head, and close my eyes. I try to get to better thoughts. Something I love to do. Or a place I love to go. No surprise, everything connects to Frenchie. He's in all my scenes. That thought takes me close to home.

Our friend Anzie Maylord owns the blueberry farm at the top of the place we call Sundrop Meadow. You could say, our big old backyard meets her big old backyard. But it's a good hike between our houses.

Pop jokes about this little piece of bad luck—that the

wild blueberries haven't managed to creep onto our part of the barrens. ("Still hoping Mother Nature will do us the favor." He says it every season.) The good luck is, we have an open invite from Anzie. July through the beginning of September, we head up with our buckets, a couple of times a week. We go in the early evening, after all the machine picking stops. We check the perimeter where berries get left behind. But handpicking in the low bush is tough. We work our way up to the enclosure where Anzie keeps her cultivated high-bush berries. That's the place to fill a bucket.

Anzie is neighborly. And we are neighborly back. We bring her bread or pesto or flavored vinegar. She gives us a rosy grin every time we see her, then tosses her thick curly braid over her shoulder. But her boyfriend, Carney Huggins, who lives with her now—eh—not so neighborly. Not so welcomey.

We see him more than I want to. Sometimes more than we see Anzie because her pie-baking business keeps her in the kitchen. Carney does the pie deliveries. But he finishes early. Come afternoon, he's doing this or that around the fields. He's tall, skinny, and scruffy. Suntanned to a crisp. His hair is even messier than mine, cap on or cap off.

Carney has never chased us out. But he scowls, and looks at our buckets like we're thieves. Don't know how he got Huggins for a last name. Hard to picture him doing much hugging, though I suppose he hugs Anzie. He's mighty more friendly when the parents come with us—even if that means Cedar too, running around the fields like a miniature tornado—which he does. When I'm up there with Frenchie, I can't help hoping we won't see Carney. Helps to stay low and stick to picking.

Picking is one of the things that Frenchie gets. From the first time he watched me do it, he understood how the string on the bucket went around your neck and left you two hands to pick with. He knows ripe from not ripe, and he cleans the bushes like he's a machine. The only thing that slows him down is stopping to watch the barn swallows skimming over the field, catching bugs. Or if he sees the cedar waxwings come in for a meal. They love the blueberries. So do the deer. Natural pruners, Anzie Maylord calls them. She always shrugs and says, "I've got no grudges with the wildlife."

Might have been three weeks ago Frenchie and I were up there filling buckets with berries to bring home for freezing. I was thumbing clusters of fat blues into my bucket, slapping mosquitoes and daydreaming. Suddenly, Frenchie was on the move. I knew why. He wanted to get to Anzie's barn.

"Wait up! I'm coming!" I started trotting. I held my bucket to keep it from bumping against my belly. My backpack wobbled. I opened my mouth wide and let out a—I don't know—a sound. Like a huge yawn.

"Fuh-fuh-Frenchie! Wait for me!" I was giggling as we came alongside the big barn near Anzie's house. The barn is covered in rows and rows of old shingles. There are words painted on the side of the barn in big white block letters. It's a poem that Anzie wrote:

SUN RAIN WIND SWEPT
BUD BLOSSOM BERRY
SWEET EARTH ROOTS KEPT
MAKE A SOUL MERRY

Every time we reach the barn, Frenchie stops. He waits for me to read. I used to go right up to his ear and say "S-s-sun," because I liked the way Frenchie brought his shoulder up when my breath tickled him. I'm a pest. I confess. But there was more to it. When I said "S-s-sun r-r-rain w-w-wind sw-wept" into Frenchie's ear, I was trying to put the words into him.

But I know his ear is not some sort of tunnel into the depths of him. One day I realized something so big I had to say it out loud—so I would hear it. "Why do you want to do that anyway, Aurora Pauline Petrequin? Why change him? He's perfect. Perfectly Frenchie."

I caught up to him—I always do—and stood beside him. We faced the side of the barn, I took a huge breath and recited the poem—loudly.

"'Sun rain wind swept. Bud blossom berry. Sweet

earth roots kept. Make a soul merry!'" I threw my arms wide. I shook out my shoulders. I took another breath. I was ready to go again when I heard—

"Aurora!" There stood Carney Huggins, backward cap and one eye closed like he might have a headache.

I popped my eyes open. Carney knew my name? Could not believe that!

"Be quiet." He pushed the words at me. Stuck a hard *t* sound on the end. He sighed. Then for a second or two it seemed like Carney Huggins looked past me, to where Frenchie stood still, staring at the poem on the barn. First time I ever saw Carney really look *at* Frenchie, and for once, Carney's face didn't look so cranky. I should have let that moment last longer.

"Sorry for being too loud," I said. "Frenchie likes the poem—"

"Yeah, that's fine." Carney looked back at me, scowling again. "But do you have to shout it?"

"Uh . . . well . . . no. But maybe it'll scare the fruit flies off the berries if I do," I offered.

His shoulders sagged.

"Or not," I said.

"Are you done picking?" He stuck his chin toward my bucket. "Late season, you know. Not much left. And Mr. Plaid?" Carney actually smiled for a second. "Looks like he did all right. How about you head out, now." He gave his head a little swing toward the back of the property.

"Oh! Not so fast," I said. I turned to show him my backpack. "Mom and Pop sent two loaves of sourdough for Anzie. And you too. I guess."

"That's really nice," he said, but he sounded like he had a stomach cramp. "Drop them off at the kitchen. Quietly, if you can. Huh?"

"Sure," I said, "anything to make your soul merry." I jumped and pointed at the barn. Almost spilled my berry bucket. I gave him a grin.

"Shh!" Carney shook his head once more.

"Oops, sorry. Too loud."

He turned away and set off for Anzie's vegetable patch. I turned to Frenchie and whispered, "Come on. Sheeshy-sheeshy. Nothing new there."

Frenchie followed me to Anzie's kitchen door. I pulled the two loaves of sourdough out of my pack. I decided not to knock, because maybe I'd done enough bothering. I left the bread in a delivery crate on her bench.

On the way home I told Frenchie, "Ya know, it's possible that Carney Huggins and I won't ever be a good mix. But ya know what, Frenchie? I think he kind of likes you. Maybe you're his kind of kid."

Aurora

Spotting the Spotted Deer

When I want to get outside, which is always, but Frenchie is feeling lazy or hard to reach, I make him a promise. "This will be a bird hike," I'll say. If that doesn't get him, I push harder. "Hey! This is the blue jay talking to you, Frenchie." I flap my arms. Let's get outside and fly!" That gets him up, and it's all good because we both get what we want.

About a year ago we started out on one of those bird hikes up Sundrop Meadow, not far from Anzie's. Good day for sightings. Frenchie was flapping, whistling, and tweeting every few minutes. I kept slowing to a stroll to make sure he caught up to me. I checked the ground for rocks. Nothing exciting there. I was starting to feel bored until—

On the path ahead I heard a swish. Then a clacking sound like rock against rock. A flash of white and brown streaked across the trail. I halted. So did Frenchie.

"Whu-hut . . . ," I whispered. I thought someone's goat was running loose. The animal stopped in the high grass under the twiggy trees. It turned back and looked right at us.

I caught my breath.

Not a goat.

A deer?

Yeah. Because, flyswatter ears.

But this deer was not like any I had ever seen. It was spotted from head to hoofs, with a lot of white on its coat. The tip of its nose looked extra round, like a black rubber ball. Its snout was white and broader than I'd ever seen on a whitetail, with a dark marking along the center. A pair of brown diamond-shaped patches gave the deer a perfect mask—pretty as a stuffed toy—with dark eyes shining out, and white eyebrows arching upward.

"Wow . . . ," I whispered so low. "Now, Frenchie"—I hoped he would get what I was about to say—"you don't bother with birds at a time like this!"

Then I tried not to breathe. Frenchie stood still right beside me. I was with the best, silent deer-watching person in the world. We'd seen plenty of white-tailed deer together. Enough to know they don't hang around for long. (Sometimes I wonder if they know there are a lot of hunters in Maine.)

Stay, stay. I sent that spotted deer a good hard-thinking message, and maybe that got through. Big long seconds went by while we looked each other over. The deer was small. Not the same way a fawn is small—even though I guessed it was young. This deer's body was thicker than a fawn's. Its legs were short but strong—or so I told myself. It watched us. It blinked, and it seemed unafraid.

I daydreamed: This deer had come on the path because of us—Frenchie and me. Like an end-of-summer gift. It must want to know us and take apples or sunflower seeds from our hands. (Except we didn't have any, and it wasn't quite that close. But almost.) I imagined it would let us touch its warm neck and lead us into the woods. Maybe take us to a deposit of stones, maybe to a vein full of chunks of dark green or blue tourmaline . . .

"Hello," I whispered. The deer twitched its ears. Slowly, I raised one hand, palm up. I stepped forward. A stick snapped. The deer sprang away. That spotty white coat flickered through the woods and was gone.

"Ah, dang," I said. "Sorry, Frenchie. I broke the spell." He was already heading back along the path for home. I caught up to him, passed him, and jumped in front of him. "Wait!"

Frenchie stopped.

"You saw it, right?"

Frenchie stared. Slow blink.

Come on, I thought. Tell me you saw that crazy strange deer, Frenchie.

All he did was hoist his needlepoint purse up into his armpit.

I stepped out of his way. He started walking again. I stayed behind him and mumbled, "Do you think I scared it off when I put my hand out? That was dumb of me, huh?" I followed his plaid shirt. "Weirdest creature ever. I didn't even know what it was at first. Never seen a deer like that. Never heard of a deer like that. I'll look it up though. See what I can find out."

I thought about some key words to use. "*Spotted deer. In the woods.* Oh. *State of Maine.* I guess that should be in there too, huh? I'll tell you everything I learn," I promised. "But what do you say we keep it a secret. For now?"

Easy ask.

Frenchie couldn't tell anyone about the deer. Of course, that also meant, if I went home and said I'd seen a most fantastically enchanting, rare spotted deer, and nobody believed me, Frenchie couldn't back me up either.

"Hope we see it again," I said. "Wait! I'm going to leave a marker before we get too far." I dug my heel into the ground and scratched out a big X. "Eh. Nah. A good rain will wash that right out." I picked up a thick stick, tall as me, and tried to twist it into the ground. It wouldn't go, so

I jumped on it and twirled it with all my weight, and don't you know, that stick broke and I fell. I put a big new scrape in my arm.

"Dang! Hey, Frenchie! Wait up!"

He didn't. I rubbed my bloody arm, and that stung like heck. But I couldn't care much. Not after seeing what we'd seen.

"Whoo-hoo!" I shouted. I wound my arms around like a double windmill and ran to catch up to Frenchie.

Aurora

About Piebald Deer

A few days after we saw the spotted deer, Frenchie had all his bird prints arranged on the floor like quilt squares. Corners matched up, just right. I settled beside him and inched the tips of my fingers right up close to the edge of the first row of bird prints. If I moved one, he would straighten it. (Gracia says he has a strong sense of order.)

"So," I said, "I learned all about our spotty deer. First, it's rare. Get what I'm saying? Not so many walking this earth."

I wasn't sure how much to tell him. I'm always guessing about that. But this time, it was more that I needed to talk.

"There's a sad part, Frenchie. Piebalds don't do so well. It's kind of like, if you see spots and patches on the outside, it means there's other stuff wrong on the inside. Like messed-up bones and weak organs. Piebalds don't live as long as most deer. Gets me right in my heart."

Frenchie stared at his bird pictures. He squeezed his hands into little fists.

He's listening, I thought, and he is sorry, like I am.

I flopped on my back, stared at the ceiling. "I hope we get to see the piebald again. I want to check up on it. Make sure it's okay," I said. "And if we see it, let's follow it. For as long as it'll let us. That means we can't scare it. So I won't reach at it, and you can't flap and tweet, okay? We just follow. Can you do that for me?"

Frenchie popped up off the floor and made a beeline for our kitchen. I hadn't even noticed but Pop was running the mixer. Making bread dough. Frenchie never misses that.

I rolled up on one elbow and looked at his bird pictures, laid out so perfectly. I reached for the nuthatch print, the one Frenchie got from the woman at that cinnamon-smelling shop Troviosity. There were two birds in the painting. One heading up the tree, one heading down. I turned it upside down, wondering if Frenchie would notice. When the mixer stopped, and he came back, he knew. In a millisecond. He turned the nuthatch picture right-side up.

"Okay," I whispered near his ear. "So if you get that, I'm going to count on you to get what I said about the pie-bald deer."

Frenchie pulled up his shoulder. I laughed. "You are so ear ticklish," I said.

Carney Huggins

Special Delivery

Carney Huggins was half done with the pie deliveries. He was coasting at a good clip along Punkinville Road when a strange *something* bounded out in front of him— and stopped.

It. Will. Move.

That's the last thought Carney had before he jammed on his brakes. He threw his arm in front of the stack of pie boxes on the passenger's seat beside him. A matter of reflex, that was. But in a sudden stop, everything that's not bolted down will keep going forward.

Carney did. His clipboard did. Five out of seven pies did. Even the pair of five-gallon buckets that had been riding in the bed of the pickup did. They rolled right up over the top of the cab and bounced off the hood of the truck. Now they were rolling in the road.

In the next few seconds Carney did several things. He slumped in his seat and swore. He pushed his cap back to the top of his head. He shut down his engine, *and* he smelled blueberry pie like he'd never smelled it before, which was saying a lot.

Carney blinked. He scanned the side of the road for the animal. What was that anyway? He'd seen something similar—a deer, but not a normal one—during a blinding sunset in the barrens a few days back. He'd gotten an only slightly better look today. But that *was* a deer. Had to be the same one. Peculiar as could be. Spotted, and prettier than a prizewinning pony. Or something that'd walked out of a fairy tale. Who the heck was he going to tell that to?

Carney looked around the cab of the truck. He'd managed to save only two of the pies—or so he thought. The three pie boxes that happened to be below his hand had probably hit the glove compartment. The two that happened to be above his hand must have hit the dashboard. Hardly mattered, because all five of those pie boxes had come to rest on the floor of the passenger's side of the truck. Some had their lids flung open, revealing a serious misarrangement of runny purple berries and broken golden crusts. As for the two pies Carney thought he had saved, well, a peek under each lid disclosed that they, too, had gone forward inside their boxes.

"Pie pileups," Carney muttered. Boy, did they smell good.

He popped his door and slid out of the truck. Best to get his buckets out of the road. They were still rolling side to side, seeking a level, Carney figured, and he laughed because there was nothing level about Punkinville Road. Both buckets were fatally busted. Not surprising. He set them into the bed of the pickup.

Now. What to do about the pies?

He opened the passenger's side, and the fresh-baked aroma struck him again. Ahh. Anzie did make the best blueberry pies. Carney lifted the boxes and their loose contents up onto the seat of the truck. He propped on one buttock inside the open door. The pies were unsalable . . . but not inedible.

Hand pies.

That's what Carney thought as he slid his fingers under a nice half-sandwich-size pocket of crust. Deftly, he dumped the oozing berry filling into his mouth and folded the pastry in after it. As he savored that cheekful, he glanced out through the truck's back window. He thought he saw something—a flash of plaid, was it? Plaid on Punkinville Road could only mean someone was around, and here he was in an embarrassing mess of pies and broken buckets. He was in no mood to chat. He stayed low, pushed another scrap of pie into his mouth. He snuck a few more peeks out the truck windows. Where did that plaid go? Had his eyes played a trick?

Some minutes later Carney was either sick of pie or about to be sick because of pie. He sucked purple syrup off his thumb. Time to go back and find out what Anzie wanted to do about the failed delivery. On the way he'd think how to describe the weird deer that had caused all the trouble this morning.

Carney shut the passenger's side door. He used his elbow and his shirtsleeve to polish the dust off the painted side of the truck. The letters spelled out Anzie's poem. That's what she called it—a poem. Carney wasn't so sure, though it hardly mattered. He did so love Anzie. But alone on Punkinville Road he had a few thoughts, such as, Wasn't it more a list of words? Could a list be a poem? Anzie sure thought so. She'd put it on everything that had anything to do with the farm, including the long barn, including this truck.

SUN RAIN WIND SWEPT.

He wondered, not for the first time, shouldn't that be WINDSWEPT?

BUD BLOSSOM BERRY. Okay. Yes. It was a blueberry farm, and alliteration was a happy thing.

SWEET EARTH ROOTS KEPT. Hmm. That seemed a bit out of order.

MAKE A SOUL MERRY.

"Bah," said Carney. That last line seemed especially discordant because the only way he could hear it now was the way that neighbor girl had recited it—no, screamed it—on an otherwise-serene evening.

Aurora. That was her name. She was Ed Petrequin's kid. Carney knew Ed from around town, and as a neighbor since Ed owned all that land adjacent to Anzie's and had built the A-frame down the hill. Nice enough folks, and Anzie was very fond of them. But, oh, that Aurora. And her busy little brother, whose name Carney could never remember. Birch? No. Oakley? No. But it had something to with some tree or other.

"Pine cone," he said out loud. Then he snorted a laugh, which burned of blueberry. Anyway, those Petrequin kids were out of control. Carney wasn't much of a kid person, and he knew it, which is why he was surprised by the brand-new soft spot he felt for Aurora's friend—the boy who didn't talk. Wasn't that all kinds of ironic? The quietest kid he'd ever run across paired with the loudest one on earth? Carney remembered looking at the boy as he'd stared at Anzie's poem on the side of the barn. Unremarkable pose, and Carney wasn't sure he could read. If he'd thought anything, it was that the kid had always seemed absent or empty. Wrong. That boy was taking in something from having Anzie's verse shouted at him. Carney could still see the boy's dark eyelashes closing down—that slow blink. Why did some scenes stick in the memory? Then he remembered something else about the boy: the plaid shirt.

Frenchie

The Truck

Something inside Frenchie told him it would not be good for the deer to leap just then. But it did. Into the road. It stopped and looked back at Frenchie.

The truck halted. It threw buckets at the deer.

Bump-bah-dah—bang! Bang!

The deer sprang into the woods on the other side of the road.

Frenchie could see the opening between the trees. He knew where to go. But first he watched Carney Huggins pick up the buckets and get back inside the truck.

Quiet. Quiet is what Carney likes.

Frenchie saw the words on the truck. Same as on the barn:

SUN RAIN WIND SWEPT.

He remembered.

SUN SUN SUN.

That's what Frenchie always thought should come next. But it didn't. Aurora always said something else. But she wasn't there to say it now. So Frenchie tilted his face up and thought:

SUN SUN SUN.

His nose holes filled with the scent of blueberries. Warm and heavy. The way they are when Anzie pulls them from her oven. When Ed puts them in pancakes.

SUN SUN SUN.

Frenchie crossed the road, he slipped behind the truck, in a hurry to catch up with the deer. He saw Carney Huggins sitting in the truck. Down low. Eating the warm berries.

Quiet.

Frenchie stepped into the cool slice of shade between the trees. The deer place. A thin trail. Pretty soon, he saw the spots. Pretty soon, he began to watch his feet again. Hike, hike, hike.

And still, he thought Aurora would be behind him.

SUN SUN SUN.

Aurora

Messages for Frenchie

Ms. Chandra and her students have gone back to the art room. A few more kids have stopped by to leave Post-its on the ever-changing-tree mural. I look at the handwriting—some curly, some printed, some block letters. I read the messages:

So sorry you are missing.
Come home soon, Frenchie L!
God is watching over you.
Wherever you are, I hope you are seeing some great birds.
Chirp-chirp!
Come home safe.

(I'd like to take my marker to that one. It should say *safely*.)

I think you are in my math class and we miss you there.
Dear Frenchie, we are on the lookout for you!
Hope you are warm enough.

(That one is odd. It's not even cold out.)

The messages are nice, I guess. But this is a change to the ever-changing-tree mural that I wish had never had come. I'm trying not to be sour about it, but a lot of the notes are from kids who have never bothered with Frenchie before today, kids who walk right by him in the hall—because most kids do.

There is one bright green Post-it note that says this:

I owe you an apology. Please come get it.

No one was watching when that one went up. I know for sure, because it's from me.

Aurora

A Worst Possible

This is the feeling of a Worst Possible. I mess up a lot. I say I am sorry about ten times day. Mom and Pop tell me that's okay, and to move on from those things. But a Worst Possible is bigger than that. It sticks harder. I think the only cure is a time machine. That's what I want now. I want to go back to this morning, walk through the doors of the school and *not* have Frenchie behind me. I would put him beside me, I'd get him to his classroom, and I'd see him go in.

I close down hard on my eyes. The Worst Possible wells up in me.

"Frenchie," I whisper into the air. "Where did you go?"

It happened this past July. A Worst Possible a lot like this one. I made the same mistake. I forgot what was behind me. Mom and Pop and Gracia said that Frenchie and I could take a short hike while they were making dinner. Nothing unusual about that *until* I asked if we could take Cedar, and Mom and Pop said yes!

"Really? We can? Hear that, Cedar Tree? Want to go walking with Frenchie and me?" Well, my little brother headed for the door. He was going to get out before someone changed their mind. "Frenchie, come on!" I said, jumping up and down. Frenchie and I were the big kids. Apparently, we could be trusted. Especially me.

I've always tried to help with Cedar. I've done everything I can for him, including sometimes loving him up too hard and making him cranky. But I also have it in my head that I am my best self around him. Better than I am with other kids—except Frenchie; I feel pretty *best* with him too.

"Keep your eye on the little sprinter," Mom warned.

"Frenchie," Gracia said. She looked up from a platter of portobello mushrooms she was oiling for the grill. "You'll help Aurora with Cedar, yes?"

"He will," I said. "We'll be back in thirty minutes. Sound good? Okay, great." I loved answering my own questions.

"Fifteen," said Pop. "Grill's already lit."

"Okay, twenty," I said, "and we'll stay where we can *smell* dinner cooking. How's that?"

"Fairly reasonable," Pop said. "Twenty minutes, then." He pulled his phone out of his pocket. He set the timer, then held it out to me.

"When it rings, start back home," he said. "And, Aurora, I don't need to say it, do I?"

"Yeah, yeah. Take good care of the phone."

"No!" He scoffed. "Take good care of Cedar!"

"Oh! Right!"

What a feeling that was, walking out with Frenchie *and* Cedar, with Pop's phone swinging in the deep pocket of my shorts. Cedar didn't even look back. He wrapped all his little fingers around three of mine and off we went, with Frenchie a little way behind us. I knew we could make it to the crest and catch those couple of minutes when the sun goes low and the tree trunks are all lit up and glowing on their west-facing sides.

Sure enough we did.

"Look at that. Looks like the trees are on fire, doesn't it?" I said.

Neither Frenchie or Cedar could give me much of an answer. But Cedar was in a big-boy mood without our parents. He nodded his head like he understood. Frenchie stared and blinked a little.

"When I see the light do that, that's when I start to get

what artists do," I said. "Light and dark make shapes, but also, I think shape is the reason you see light and dark. Something like that. . . ."

"Yah," said Cedar, nodding again. "Yah, Awoh-wah."

I loved him so much for trying to use his words. But most of the talking was up to me, of course. As we walked, I said, "Feel that? How it's warmer down around your legs? The grass is holding on to all the heat from the sun today. But up here"—I swung Cedar's arm up—"the air is cooler." Cedar turned his chin up at me and giggled. I let his arm down again. "It's like the grass was baking all day. Like bread. You can even smell it." I gave the air a big sniff.

Cedar tried to do the same, but he did what he always does; he blew out instead. I folded over, laughing. Then Cedar laughed too. Frenchie stared ahead, and that was one of those times I wished he could get what laughing is—the unstoppable way it happens.

I used the hem of my tank top to wipe Cedar's nose. He stood for it way better than usual. "Good job, Cedar. I think we got it all. What do you think, Frenchie?" I looked and he was doing the stare. Like he was actually seeing something. I looked where Frenchie was looking and—zow! Right there in front of us, no more than the space between first base and second base, stood the piebald deer. Again!

"Ooo!" I whispered. "Down! Down! Get low." I tugged

139

on Cedar. Not hard. Frenchie dropped too. There we were on our bellies and elbows.

"Look, Cedar. See that deer? See the spots? And all those colors? That is called a *piebald* deer."

Cedar blinked as he peeked through the grasses. The deer picked up its head. "Shh . . ." I put my finger on my lips, and Cedar folded his lips in. The deer went back to grazing. Every so often its ears flicked at a halo of bugs.

"Oh, he's a boy," I whispered. "Nubs up top. He's got baby antlers."

The three of us lay still, watching, even Cedar.

"Cedar Tree," I whispered. "Don't ever forget this, okay? Don't forget that you got to see a piebald deer." Would he remember? Could he? What did I remember from being two and half years old? Not so much. "Try, Cedar. Try not to forget."

"'Kay, Awoh-wah," he whispered.

The deer raised his head again. Then he began to walk.

"We've got to follow," I said. "Stay low." Frenchie wasn't much for crouching, but Cedar did what I did. We walked into the ferns, leaving about twenty feet between us and the deer. The low light caught his coat as he headed into the woods. He had at least as many colors on him as Anzie Maylord's calico barn cat.

I looked behind me and motioned for Cedar to keep coming. He was holding back a grin, as if smiling might make too much noise. The deer hopped over a fallen pine branch. I wove a path between the skinny trees, hugged my way around the boulders. I looked back and saw Frenchie standing tall, stepping along. I kept following that piebald, stopping whenever he stopped, my heart beating hard. We'd never been able to follow the deer for so long. I scratched a bug bite while I drank in the sight of him. He was weird and beautiful, and he was *letting* us be this close, and—

Brr-ba-ding! Brr-ba-ding!

I jumped right out of my mosquito-bitten skin. The deer raised his head, then leaped.

Brr-ba-ding! Brr-ba-ding!

Pop's phone buzzed and rang and buzzed and rang. I jammed my hand into my pocket and yanked the phone out. I shut down the alarm. I growled. Then I roared. The piebald was gone.

"Can you believe that?" I said. I turned around to face Frenchie and Cedar. "Darn it!" I stamped a foot down and cracked a dry stick. Frenchie stood, tall and plaid, and stared at one of those non-places off behind me, and Cedar—where was Cedar?

"Cedar!" I stood on my toes, looking over into the ferns and grasses. "Cedar Tree?" I could *not* see him. And right then is when my heart felt like it was puking inside of me—the Worst Possible filling my insides. "Oh my—Cedar!" I called. "Frenchie! Wh-where is he? Where?"

Of course, Frenchie just stood there, opening and

141

closing his hands. This was up to me. I suddenly had no idea how far I had tracked the piebald.

It was only minutes. Not far. Right?

I couldn't think when I had last turned to check on Cedar. *My tiny little brother!*

I scrambled to the top of a high rock. I scanned the woods and called for Cedar. Why wasn't he answering? "Cedar? I have a game for you! Say my name!" I had never heard so much silence. "Cedar, if you can hear me! Say my name right now!"

And he did. And when he did, Frenchie started walking toward him. And I started breathing again. I jumped down and crashed over dead branches to get to him, scraped my legs in the puckabrush and didn't care one bit.

Cedar was fine. He wasn't far away, crouching low in the ferns. A little nest. I hugged the heck out of him. He looked at me with big round eyes.

"'Kay, Awoh-wah?" he said. It sounded like a question, so I answered.

"Yeah, yeah. I'm okay." But I had to hold back tears. That never happens to me. I sniffed hard. "Hey, come on, you guys. We better hustle home."

I put Cedar on my back. Hitched his little legs under my arms. I brushed a tiny trickle of blood from a scratch on his shin. "You're okay, you're okay," I told him.

Frenchie walked us out of the woods. I called up to

thank him. He always knows where he's going. He made it home first, like always.

The thing about a Worst Possible is, even when it's over, if you let yourself think back on it—even for a second—it gets you all over again.

And it always will.

Aurora

Waiting with Mrs. Whilmer

Mom and Pop, where are you? Come on, come on!

I stare at the ceiling tiles in the school office, and I wonder if I can stand another minute. I tell myself, Stay positive!

I think of all the things that Frenchie knows that can keep him safe.

He can swim....

He knows how to cross the road....

He's a strong, fast walker....

Uh-oh. If Frenchie is out there fast-walking, he could be pretty far away by now. But what would ever make him do that? This morning is not a typical Frenchie morning.

Mrs. Whilmer swishes in.

"How are you doing, Aurora?" she asks. "Need anything? Can I get you a snack?"

"No, thanks," I say. "I just wish my parents would get here. And Gracia too."

Then I cover my face and think, Oh, Gracia! What will she say to me? My heart sinks—in a backward way, like it's going to hit my spine from the inside.

"They will be here soon," Mrs. Whilmer says. She glances at her watch.

"Yeah . . . I know." I dig my fingers into the sides of my face and work my cheeks like putty. "This is what an eternity is," I say. I pull up my feet and wrap my arms around my knees. Then I wiggle and reach into my pocket and pull out my geode. I squeeze it in my hands until the crystals pinch me.

Mrs. Whilmer covers my hand with hers, but then she leaves it too long. I'm uncomfortable. I do the only thing I can think of: I take back my hand, open my palm, and show her.

"Oh, a geode! And it's a beauty," she says.

"Frenchie and I split it," I tell her. I stare into its shiny center and wonder, Where's the other half now?

Aurora

Reedie's Rock Shop

The geode is new. We drove to Reedie's Rock Shop in Verona Island on Labor Day Saturday. The trip was for me, the rock hound with an allowance to spend. I planned to zero in on the tourmaline. But when I saw the geodes in a crate by the cash register, I bought one on the spot.

The whole idea with a geode is to open it, and Reedie's is all set up for that. The girl in the shop brought me the safety glasses, the chisel, and the ball-peen hammer. Frenchie knew I was going to crack that geode. He did not approve.

Everything about his body told me so. He blinked with his eyes looking up hard to his left. His chin jutted forward—the *no* pose. In case that message wasn't clear enough, he went right out the open door and stood beside the car, looking up into the trees.

"Frenchie. Come back in. Please! It'll be all right!" I called to him from the steps. He didn't budge. I leaned on the jamb, cupping the geode in both hands. It was about the size of a medium russet potato, and it looked like one too. I rubbed the dry brown surface with my thumb and wiped the dust on my shorts. I turned the geode over a few times.

Reedie's couldn't tell me where it'd come from.

"A rock shop worth its salt ought to know," I'd told the girl at the counter before I'd paid.

She'd said, "Maybe Missouri, because the riverbeds are full of them and they come up after storms."

"But you aren't sure, are you?" I'd said. And she said no, she was not.

But I'd made my choice, and I wanted to split it and find out what kind of crystals had formed inside of it. All Frenchie wanted was to get back in the car.

I looked over my shoulder into the shop. Mom and Gracia and Cedar were stopping beside barrels of tumbled stones.

"Ahhh! Yocks!" said Cedar. He pushed both his little hands deep into a barrel of polished pink quartz.

"Yes. R-r-rocks," I heard Mom pronouncing it for him. "Scoop. But don't throw, Cedar boy," she added.

Gracia leaned into Mom with something in her hand. "Rene, look at this blue one with the black and white veins running through it. What is this?" Together they searched for a label.

"Sodalite," I called from the door.

"Oh, good guess, Aurora!" Mom called. "You're right."

I shrugged. Had I wasted several weeks' allowance on a rock-hard potato? Yeah, I was a geode owner for the first time in my life. That was pretty cool, even though it was store-bought. But I'd had a special reason for buying it, and if Frenchie wasn't into this, it was going to bum me right out. I don't spend for rocks easily. Buying seems like cheating. If I add a rock, I want to be the person who found it.

Pop had once said, "Aurora, your rules for rock hunting could make for a small accumulation."

I had told Pop, "I am planning to grow at least as old as you. I have years of searching ahead of me. Someday, I'll ride my bike all the way to Androscoggin County for a real mineral hunt. Someday, I'll borrow the car from you and Mom and drive all the way to the state of Oregon to look for thunder eggs."

Pop had thrown his arms over his chest and pretended to faint onto our couch. All six foot six of him, laid out, with big work boots hanging over the armrest.

The memory made me snort as I stood in the doorway watching Frenchie.

"Hey," I called. "It's not really breaking it; it's more like opening it. Something amazing could be on the inside. Shiny stuff." It probably wasn't worth telling him all the fun facts about geodes, like how it takes decades for one to form, and how you never know what sorts of crystals might be lining the hollow—anything from quartz to purple amethyst. Even agates and jaspers. I wasn't about to lie and say a bird would come flying out, but I thought about it.

"I got it so we could share it." I told him. "I figure we'll each have a half to take to our new sixth-grade classrooms since we're not together this year. It'll be two things that fit right together even though they are apart. Ya know?"

Frenchie turned from the car to face me, though as usual, he didn't really look at me.

"I'll take the smaller half," I promised. Then I rolled my eyes. "Well, there you go. That's a sentence that makes no sense. If they were actually halves, they'd be the same size. That's not too likely to happen. Geodes break where they want to break. But I'll try for equals, Frenchie, and if I blow it, you can have the bigger one. Promise."

And that's when he came back inside Reedie's Rock Shop.

I was not going to let him change his mind. I stuck the safety glasses on my face and set right to tapping a line into that potato-looking geode. Mom took a video of the whole thing. That's how I know what my breath sounded like when the geode fell into two pieces. You can hear me say, "Aww! It's a beauty! Nice crystal cavity. And look! Look! We got ourselves a snowball burr on one side! See that nice round part in there?" Mom followed me with her phone as I leaned toward Frenchie. "Oh! And another! One in each piece. I don't think that happens a lot." I said it right to the camera. "This second one's pretty tiny. See? But I'd say that's still a *snowball*."

Then you can hear Cedar say, "No-baw! No-baw!" He leans forward, and before any of us can stop him, he sticks the tip of his tongue into the bigger geode half and gives it a lick!

The picture goes tilty and blurry, and you can hear Mom laughing. Gracia too. And me, being so happy that Frenchie went along with cracking the geode.

We ran our pinkies all along the cavities, and felt the edges of the crystals. We looked at both pieces with magnifying glasses. Then I slid the larger piece of the geode across the top of the hammered-up table at Reedie's until it sat right in front of Frenchie with all its crystals shining up at him.

"Yours," I said. Then he reached for both pieces of the geode. Slowly, he fitted them back together like he was fixing a broken egg. Frenchie gets stuff, but I didn't expect that. Neither did Gracia. She got teary. Then he held the smaller piece close to his chest and pushed the larger one in front of me.

"Me?" I said. "You want me to have the bigger piece?"

Frenchie didn't speak. But he did answer. In a very Frenchie way. He opened the flap on his needlepoint purse and dropped the small half of our geode inside. Then he walked back out of Reedie's Rock Shop and stood beside the car again, ready to go home.

Aurora

The Glue

Mom, Pop, Gracia, and Cedar *finally* walk through the front door at Mountain View School. I slither off my orange chair to the floor, then bounce to my feet. I peel around the glass partition and fall against them all. We hug—oh my gosh, we hug! It's not that perfectly happy sort of hugging. It's more like, time to glue ourselves together. We are all going to find Frenchie.

I see how much Gracia needs him back. She presses her palms together and takes shivery breaths. There is a little crying but no apologizing—no time for that. The town is taking over the search for Frenchie. They are setting up headquarters down at the Fire and Rec Center. We need to be there.

I run for the van shouting, "I'll take the way-back seat!"

I keep watch out the windows all the way down Bert Gray Road. I am looking for Frenchie, hoping to spot him, waiting in a yard or a field. The words sit ready on the tip of my tongue. I want to say them *so* much: *There! He's there!*

But I don't get to.

We drop Gracia at her house. I watch her on the step. She's hunched, like she is folding up with worry. But she straightens and flings the door open and slips inside quickly. She's going ahead of us to the Fire and Rec Center. No point in her waiting while four Petrequins get organized. Mom has to change her clothes. We'll need our boots and water bottles. We are about to start the most important hike of our lives.

"Let's hurry," I say. I rock in the seat, even though home is only yards away now. Cedar rocks too.

Mom and Pop are talking.

"We'll need the carrier for Cedar, or we'll be no help at all," Mom says.

"The carrier, diapers, and the *vests*," Pop says sharply.

"That's tomorrow," Mom says. "Archery season opens tomorrow. Designated areas only."

Oh right, I think. Orange Days. Hunting season. Every year, Mom blocks the days onto our family calendar with a neon-orange marker. Early September to

153

mid-December. Those are the days we wear bright orange safety vests for hiking *anywhere*, or even filling our own bird feeder, or raking leaves in our yard.

"Take no chances," Pop says.

Before Pop speaks again, Mom says, "Vests. Yes. Of course."

"I wonder how they're going to organize this search." It's the last thing Pop says before we hop out of the car at home.

This search.

The words sound awful to me. My guts are yuck. I want to find Frenchie so much. "I guess they'll start near the school. Since he was there this morning." I say it mostly to myself. I feel a pull inside me to go back there and look. But the place I picture him in my mind is up at the blueberry barrens. Sundrop Meadow. Our big back-yard. Maybe it's just because we go there so much. But what if it's a hunch?

I am in my boots and ready, but Mom and Pop are still putting Cedar on the potty, and finding bug repel-lent, and filling water bottles. "Hey, please can I go up to Sundrop Meadow and cross over to Anzie's?"

"Right now?" Mom breathes out. She's exasperated.

"I want to look there first."

"We can drive up. It would be good to let Anzie know—spread the word that Frenchie is—"

"No, I mean I want to hike up. I want to look for

Frenchie. He could be up there bird-watching in the woods beside the meadow. Or maybe even picking . . ." Although, I know the crop is pretty spent for the year.

"He knows the way," I say. Those words puff me up. Frenchie in the present tense. Frenchie *now*. Because he *is* now. I'm sure he is.

"Aurora, he knows the way when he starts from home," Mom says. She has her doubtful face on. "But he didn't start from home today. . . ."

"Mom, I know. I still want to look there. Please!" I say.

Pop hears me. He follows Cedar out of the bathroom. He has fresh diapers for the day tucked under his elbow.

"So you drive it; I'll hike it. Meet me in her driveway. I can't wait anymore. I can't!"

My parents look at each other.

"No harm," says Pop. "We'll meet up at Anzie's." He puts a finger up. "No meandering, Aurora."

That's all I need to hear. I am out the door. Forget hiking. I am running. A dozen sprint steps and suddenly I hear Pop hollering my name.

"Aurora! You forgot!" I turn and see him jogging toward me. He's flapping an orange vest at me.

"Sorry, Pop! Sorry!" He wraps me into the vest and hugs me, hard. I hug him back.

"See you up the hill, my girl. Love you."

"Love you, Pop!"

Aurora

My Quick Stop in the Barrens

I hike faster than normal today on my way up to Sundrop Meadow. I talk the same way I always do—even though I am alone. Usually, I have Frenchie walking beside me, never answering, of course. But his pants always swish together, and I know all the different ways he breathes. And what his burps sound like. There's that whisper of breath he takes in before he tweets like he does. Today, there is a whole lot of silence coming back at me. It's different than not hearing answers from my friend. My person. The person who chose me to be his person. It's bigger.

I hold the bottom hem of the orange vest as I go. If only Frenchie was wearing one, he'd be easier to spot.

At the top of the meadow I turn in a slow circle,

looking and looking hard as I can. I think about the math of it, and I tell myself, he'll be along this radius, or this next one. But as I come around, I haven't spotted him, so I go round again.

I look west toward Anzie's farm, south toward home. Then I head into the East Woods. But I am not going to be a dope about this. I won't go deep. I have not forgotten that I was a little bit lost here a few weeks ago, following that piebald deer. I've still got scars from crashing through the puckabrush to get to Cedar that day. That would be a bad thing to repeat, and besides, if I get lost, well, I'm one less person to go searching for Frenchie.

That makes me stop still.

"Frenchie!" I call out. "Frenchie, can you hear me? Give me a tweet! Or come on out." I wait. Nothing. "If you're hiding, stop it! If you're crouching, quit it! Stand up! Now!" First, I'm mad. Then I'm brilliant. "Hey, want to go to Anzie's and read the poem off the barn? You know the one." At the top of my lungs I holler. "'SUN RAIN WIND SWEPT BUD BLOSSOM BERRY SWEET EARTH ROOTS KEPT . . .'" I stop to take a breath. It doesn't seem right to go on and holler out the next part: MAKE A SOUL MERRY. There's nothing merry about this. I tilt my head back, push my shoulders forward. I call, "Fren-CHEE! I'll read you the rest, but you have to come with me!" I wait. I breathe again and again.

He doesn't come.

I can't stay any longer. Mom and Pop will worry. They could be at Anzie's by now. I jam my hand into the pocket of my shorts and wrap my fingers around my geode for a second. "Come on, Frenchie," I whisper.

I scan the woods one more time. Then I turn and sprint toward Anzie's farm.

Aurora

Encountering Carney

I'm going in through the gate, breathing hard, when I see Carney Huggins. He's got some rocks by his feet (nothing special, I'm pretty sure) and a shovel in his hands. He's plugging up a gopher hole. He stops digging and squints at me.

"Hey," I say as I get near, but I try not to slow down. "Weird seeing me here this time of day, isn't it?"

He pulls his chin under. Looks like he is thinking that over. "Yeah, I guess. It is."

"Well, it's due to something bad," I tell him. "He's gone missing. In case you haven't heard." I'm still on the move, trying to sweep on by. I do *not* have time to chat with Carney.

"Wait, wait. Say again?" he says.

Now I do have to stop. "Frenchie Livernois," I say. "You know him. Comes up here with me all the time."

Carney raises one arm, reaches to scratch under the back of his hat. He's got a long purple stain running from his wrist to his bony elbow. Now that I am standing still, and kind of close to him, I am pretty sure he smells like blueberry pie. Maybe that's what he and Anzie eat for breakfast. Pie. Or maybe his clothes fill up with the smell of them when he's driving deliveries.

"Seems like he left the schoolyard early this morning," I say. "First thing."

Now Carney tilts his head. Looks like he has a question but he's not getting around to asking it.

"There's going to be a search. We'll use all the help we get," I say.

"Oh. I might . . . uh—"

"Yeah, yeah," I interrupt. "If you can't search, then spread the word. Tell three people and ask them to tell three more. Get the math? I think you kind of like him. Not me. But him. And that's okay. A lot of people think I'm too much."

"So, wait. There's a search, you say?"

"Yep." I point toward the farmhouse. "My parents are letting Anzie know. I'm here to meet them. We're going down to the Fire and Rec Center to get our assignment.

NOW." I finish up loud hoping he'll get the point. I have to go!

"Aurora!"

"What?" I turn, but I keep trotting backward. Carney Huggins has his hands cupped around his mouth like he's going to yell something at me. Sheesh, Carney! And you think I drive you nuts? Think it's easy running backward? Think I'm not worried about my friend?

"What school?" he calls. "Where did he leave from?"

"The elementary!"

"Where's that?"

"Up Bert Gray Road!" I scream back. Under my breath I say, "How can you live here and not know that?"

Maxine Grindel

Maxine and Dudley at the Hospital

Maxine Grindel sat in a chair in the exam room at the walk-in clinic. Best not to wait up on that high table, lest she get woozy again and tip over. Dudley might not be quick enough to catch her.

A nurse had firmly instructed Maxine to hold her hand high, above her heart, and to apply pressure on the end of that ring finger, which had bled through a wad of paper towels—and was *throbbing*.

It'd been over an hour since Dudley had packed Maxine—half-passed-out—into the passenger's side of the Mrs. Thrift camper van. It made sense to drive the van to the clinic; it had a new fan belt and was running like a dream.

"Where is that doctor?" Maxine's patience was eroding.

Finally, a woman who was much too young to be anybody's doctor arrived and snapped a pair of rubber gloves on. She took a good look under Maxine's clump of bloodied paper towels.

There was good news: Maxine's topless ring finger would heal, as long she followed instructions to the letter. The doctor predicted, that when all was said and done, the healed finger would look only the littlest bit misshapen, and only to someone who was really giving it a look.

"Don't care what it looks like!" Maxine exclaimed. "I need to be able to use the dang thing! I have work to do! And by the way, it *hurts!*"

The doctor gave Maxine two pills for the pain, then slipped out of the room. Again, Maxine and Dudley waited.

"It's a pity," Dudley said. He rested his hand gently on his wife's knee. "I'll miss that little bit of your finger, Maxie."

"Well, when we get home, you can look for it. Find it, and it's yours," Maxine said.

Dudley chuckled his best chuckle.

The doctor swished back in. "Starting to feel better?" she asked, her sweet young head tilted in sympathy.

Seconds later, she poured a *stinging fire* of antiseptic on Maxine's wound. Maxine moaned and thunked her forehead on Dudley's shoulder. The doctor set to wrapping Maxine's finger in cloth, followed by several layers of snowy-white gauze. Maxine watched as the doctor worked, going around and around the finger until, to Maxine's sleepy eyes, her finger had become triple-thick. Maxine started to laugh.

"Look, Dudley! I've got a little finger puppet." She wiggled it. (It didn't hurt anymore.) Maxine laughed harder.

"Don't be swinging it around, now," Dudley warned. Maxine ignored him.

"I think I'll call her Miss Mummy." She made the finger bob and bow. "Hello, hello! Do you like this show? No!" She tilted her head back and cackled.

A short time later, Maxine was half-asleep on the bench outside the clinic with Miss Mummy resting in her lap. The September sun warmed her face. Dudley had gone to get the camper van from the parking lot. Maxine heard the engine rev up in the distance.

The Mrs. Thrift-mobile, she thought, and she smiled because that new fan belt sounded so right.

Maxine waited. She observed a few cars out on Dixon Way. Watched the garbage truck backing up over at the Dental Associates building. *Beep-beep-beep.* It was a terrible noise. But everything seemed pleasant to Maxine.

Soon, she heard voices nearby. Folks standing in the circle right beside her. Maxine narrowed her eyes. Were those uniforms? Looked like it.

"There's a missing boy . . . ," someone said.

"We're heading out to join now . . . the search . . . underway . . ."

Maxine tried very hard to tune in.

"Sixth grader," she heard. "So, how old is that? Ten or eleven?"

Maxine knew the answer. She tried to speak. She might have said, "Eleben." Then "Whu-bere?" and "Whu is dis do say?" Then she might have asked, "Whu-appened?"

The uniforms were not answering. Maxine listened harder.

"Poor kid. . . . There's something about him. . . . They say he doesn't talk."

Wait . . .

A thought bubbled up in her head. Didn't she know a boy who didn't talk? Maxine's eyebrows arched. Oh, but her lids felt heavy. And Lord, she was tired.

The camper van rolled to a stop right in front of her. And there was Dudley, sweet old Dudley, helping her up and in.

On the way home Maxine wondered many things. Why didn't her finger hurt anymore? Why was her mind floating through with thoughts of that boy . . . *Frenchie?*

165

Frenchie, who's momma had bought him the needlepoint purse. Maxine slowly remembered the day. Baker's Field. Right off Route 1. Hotter than a Tater Tot. Horrid with buzzing flies. Hmm. Last July? Or the one before?

Jewell Laramie

Stuck in Traffic

Jewell Laramie had everything she needed for her soft-ball league's end-of-season picnic. She liked to wrap up with a decent celebration, and she always chose the first Friday in September. Fact was, Jewell found endings rather bittersweet. Best way to get through? Have a party! Tonight was the night.

She was nearly back to town, having spent the morning packing her Jeep with paper plates, napkins, and red-checked tablecloths. She'd been to the Picklonious Deli—league sponsor—where she'd fetched gallon-size jugs of sweet relish, mustard, ketchup, *and* three huge jars of famous Picklonious sour pickles.

"Lot of vinegar in the Jeepy today." Jewell had joked

with Sid and Berkley from the deli as they'd shouldered the jars and jugs to her car.

Jewell had thought it all through—how to pack the back of her Jeep in a particular order. The boxes of soft-ball mini trophies—which she'd purchased on her own dime—were already snugged up against her bow and quiver, which were mounted on the rack behind the Jeep's rear seat (another end-of-summer ritual). The paper goods and condiments were nestled in next. The two coolers full of hot dogs, slaw, and potato salad—currently filling up Jewell's fridge—would fit in the center, and the three large bags of charcoal would go in last because she'd need them first.

Yep. Jewell Laramie knew how to be efficient.

It would've been nice if she could have trusted someone else to fire the grills. But Jewell believed that if she wanted this celebration done right, she had best do it herself.

As she reached the center of town, traffic moved in that slow, parade-like way that was typical of Maine in summertime. "Even post–Labor Day weekend," she muttered. "Well, this is *Vacationland*." Maine license plates had been embossed with the slogan. "Since 1936! Fun fact." Jewell chuckled and waggled a finger in the air.

She hovered her foot over her brake pedal, pressing down as needed. The traffic crept along, in barely broken, bumper-to-bumper stretches in both directions. When

Jewell reached the Fire and Rec Center, the two cars in front of her took righthand turns into the lot. She gave the place a glance as she let her Jeep snail forward. Lot of activity—

HONK-honk-honk!

Jewell hit the brakes. Her blood rushed. An insistent old Chevy in the oncoming lane turned in front of her. A second car tailed the first, as if hitched together. That driver waved to Jewell as if to say, *Yut, cutting you off! Thanks!*

Jewell set her foot on the gas. She powered forward a few yards before another car could attempt to cut across.

"Perfectly lawful on my part," she said. She shot a last look into the Fire and Rec parking lot. Maybe she could make a little stern eye contact with that pair of blockheads. Instead, she noted a whole lot of folks standing around outside the building.

Huh.

Jewell focused on the road home again, but she had a feeling now, and it nagged her. Something out of the ordinary was going on in her little part of *Vacationland*.

Oh, there! She recognized the Petrequin minivan, coming toward her. Jewell lowered her window to flag them, thinking there'd be time for a neighborly ask: Where the heck is everyone going? As they got close Jewell noticed that Rene was driving, and that her eyes were fixed on the road ahead. Ed, too, was leaning forward in a purposeful way in the passenger's seat, as if they needed to be somewhere. The van rolled on by.

Jewell wondered if they had the kiddos with them. Neat family, they were. Jewell often thought about the day they'd met. The Petrequins had turned down her offering: a beautiful venison tenderloin. They'd made it clear; they didn't eat mammals, *and* they didn't fancy hunting. Jewell chose not to be offended.

However, she thought about Aurora—all the dang time. Oh, how she had wanted that kiddo for her team—still did! "Great throwing arm. Not going to give up on that one," she said out loud. Jewell was sure that girl would mature into an excellent player. *More raw talent in her pinkie finger than I ever had in my whole body. . . .* She mused.

Jewell grinned, remembering what the girl had told her back in March when Jewell had, for the third straight year, come recruiting at the Petrequins' place.

"Trust me, Coach. You're better off without me." Aurora had flapped a hand. "I'll be scratching bug bites in your outfield and crawling out of your dugout, heading for the monkey bars between ups." Then she'd said, "Softball. Ugh! Too much standing around!" Aurora had faked a loud yawn to drive her point. Hard for Jewell to keep a straight face. Aurora had lasted almost four games the one season she did play. Jewell still cracked up every time she remembered the last one. Aurora had managed to stuff several softballs into the deep pockets of her shorts. She'd waddled onto the field for the start of the third inning, shorts sliding severely to the south.

Jewell slapped a hand down on her steering wheel in the Jeep, and sighed. "Ohh . . . what a kiddo!"

Once again, traffic slowed in front of her. She stepped on her brake pedal, stretched up and glanced in her rearview. She spotted the back of the Petrequin van, turn signal flashing cherry bright.

"By golly . . . they're heading to the Fire and Rec Center too," Jewell said.

There happened to be a slim opening in the stream of oncoming vehicles. Jewell Laramie, pulled a tight U-ey and joined the caravan.

Aurora

How to Organize a Search

At the Fire and Rec Center there is a lot of standing around. Never seen such a swarm of orange safety vests in one place. Hunting season coming. People are playing it safe. This is a different kind of hunt, I think. This is the hunt for Frenchie.

I catch sight of Coach Jewell as she pulls into the lot in her Jeep. "Huh. And here we are, standing around. Like at a softball game," I mutter. But I am glad to see her. She knows the woods, and since the woods are all around us, and Frenchie hasn't been seen anywhere else, there's a good chance he is in them. But where?

I'm standing alone because Mom and Pop (with Cedar on his back) and Gracia are at one of the check-in tables that have been set up. They are calling it headquarters. Everyone is to pick up a map, instructions, and a water bottle if they need one. I get the feeling the rescue organizers have some ideas about where to look for Frenchie. As if there are only a few places all lost kids end up.

My heart keeps taking down dives. I keep hauling it back up.

Chief Nash has a megaphone in one hand, and notes in the other. He looks like he's about to make an announcement. I do a slow 360 where I am standing. It's too much for me that so many people have turned out. It makes this real. This is a Worst Possible. I swallow hard.

Chief Nash's voice booms, "Folks! Folks! Your attention, please! May I?"

Everyone quiets down. They look up from their maps to listen.

"Thanks, people. We are grateful you are here. We have a few things to cover. Then we'll turn our parties out to various locations of interest."

"Time's a-wasting!" someone shouts.

"Giddyap!" shouts another.

Chief Nash puts up a hand, keeps his cool. "Now, we ask that you take note of some information." He turns to a pair of whiteboards set up on risers where everyone can see them. Written across the top of the first board are the words WHAT WE KNOW. Chief Nash reads them out loud, then shakes his head.

"We wish we knew more." He draws a line under the words. "Now, we are looking for our eleven-year-old boy." He begins to make a list.

BOY. 11 YEARS OLD.

"His name is Frenchie Livernois." Up goes Frenchie's name. "He is nonvocal, folks. Does. Not. Speak." He writes that down, then taps the board with the tip of his marker. "He can hear. So we want to use his name when we are out there."

I try to picture "out there." I can't see it but it feels huge—beyond huge. I wonder what searching will be like.

"He was last seen at the Mountain View School on Bert Gray Road at approximately seven forty-three this morning." He adds to the list, then says, "We know that he entered the building. For some reason, he did not enter his classroom."

For some reason named *me*, I think. I wait for Chief Nash to say it: *Aurora Pauline Petrequin*. She messed up. Forgot her best friend.

"The school has been thoroughly searched. We have determined that he is not in the building." He mentions Frenchie's clothes and backpack and the needlepoint purse. And birds. He asks if anyone has seen anything this morning—anything at all. A boy on his own. An abandoned backpack. "Please come talk to us," he says. "Even if it didn't seem important at the time. I can't stress that enough."

I am looking at my feet now. I scuff them around in the grit. When I look up, Darleen Dombroski's face is in my face. Right away, I think it: Here's something I don't need. Somehow, I keep from blurting it.

"Hi, Aurora," she says. She's got her hands behind her back. She swings her body from side to side.

"Hi." One-word answers are about all I have. I glance up at the sky, trying to avoid eye contact with Darleen. There is one of those perfect September suns straight overhead. I look down again. Darleen is still here.

"I bet you feel terrible," she says, still swinging.

"I want to find Frenchie," I say.

"We're going to help," she says. "My mom came and took me out of school early, just for this."

I nod at her.

"Nice," I say, because it is nice. Then I want to say, *What the heck, Darleen? Not like you ever did anything but screw your face up at Frenchie Livernois before today.* But I don't because we need searchers.

"We'll find him," I say. I would like to weasel away from her now, but there are people everywhere. I feel stuck. Darleen gives a little shrug.

"My mom said it'll be a good lesson."

"Lesson?" I stare at her.

"Yeah. Seeing how a search works. I've never seen what they do. I mean, of course we want to find him—"

"A lesson?" I say it again. "Are you kidding me? Frenchie

is a person. You don't get to make a lesson out of him! A lesson is a hip-hop class!" I sputter. "Or learning to knit a *s-s-something*!"

Two seconds, and there it is. The Darleen crumple face. She is going to cry. I don't get to see that through because she goes shoulder-shoving through the crowd, bouncing off people on her way. I figure she will be back. With her mother. That's another thing I don't need today.

I get a little mercy when Mom and Pop and Cedar and Gracia come to get me. "We are starting up at the school," Mom says. She waves a paper map.

As we hurry to our car, Gracia asks, "Did the app load?"

"We're loading an app?" I say. "Now? What for?"

"It's a search-party tool," Pop says as he leans into the car and settles Cedar into his seat.

"Oh. Really?"

"Yes, it's genius!" Moms says. "They asked all the volunteers to purchase it. For a few bucks, it creates a digital map and tracks us. So there will be a record of where everyone has walked, and what time each area was searched."

"Oh . . . ," I say, I think I hear my own voice brighten a little. "That's pretty cool, huh?"

"If the data show that we are retracing the steps of others, they can drop us a digital pin," says Gracia. "We'll move to an area that hasn't been covered. It should be very helpful." Her voice seems a little stronger now too.

Still, she rubs the knobs of her knuckles into her palms.

Pop gets Cedar buckled up and hands me the phone. "Watch for the download, Aurora."

I look closely at the screen.

"It's got about a quarter of the way to go," I say.

Mom and Pop hurry to the front seats while I jump into the van on one side of Cedar and Gracia goes around and slips in on the other.

I buckle in and hold the phone tighter, as if I have the power in me to speed up the download. Come on, phone, come on! Gracia needs this. We all need this. I lean around Cedar and give her a smile.

"It's happening," I say. "The dot is filling."

Before it is even done loading, and before we know if it will even work, the app seems like the greatest invention ever; it's something to believe in. Right now.

"You ready, Cedar Tree?" I say. "We're going to take a *big* hike. Going to look for Frenchie."

"En-chee," he says. His word for Frenchie.

"That's right," I say. "Frenchie." It must seem strange to Cedar that Frenchie isn't with us in the minivan right now. We are always together. Always!

"Bye-baw!" says Cedar.

He's kicks his feet and bounces. Pop turns in the passenger's seat and tells him, "Take it easy, Cedar. Easy."

Mom pulls our van out of the fire station lot, while more volunteers roll in.

"Wow. See that?" Pop says. "No doubt, we will be joined by others up at the school."

"No doubt," says Mom. She presses the gas pedal. We head off toward Bert Gray Road.

Topher Menkis

Good Intentions

Topher Menkis sat in Frenchie's chair, devastated but desperately trying to buck up. Last thing he needed was for administration to be worried about him. There was a kid to find! His plan was to hydrate and eat something, but the almond butter with apples and honey on flax bread didn't look as good as it had when he'd assembled it early that morning.

Topher had unique skills to offer for the search, *and* he had called for backup: two friends on their way. But he had to pull himself together mentally, or he'd be useless.

He looked at the collage of bird pictures taped to the top of the boy's desk in front of him. They'd made that together. Topher had brought Frenchie a new paper cutout of a feathered friend each day since the first day of school. For his part, Frenchie loved to pull out long pieces of Scotch tape, snap them off the roll, and use them to stick the birds down. They'd already gone through a whole roll of tape.

"Bird of the Day!" Topher would announce, and there were signs that Frenchie was beginning to anticipate this. That was progress. Maybe it was true that birds were the way into this silent, seemingly closed-off boy. Topher was determined to reach Frenchie. New job. Good intentions.

Now Topher tucked two fingers into his shirt pocket and tweezed out the would-be Bird of the Day, a green-eyed vireo, clipped from an old *National Geographic* magazine. He turned it over in his fingers, then let it fall onto the desk.

How had day seven become so nightmarish?

How had he lost the kid? A vulnerable kid!

Topher felt 100 percent responsible. His job was to focus on *one* boy, to encourage him and protect him.

All day.

Every day.

Topher slammed his hand flat on Frenchie's desktop.

Fail!

Aurora

The Search Begins

Mom pulls our van into the school parking lot. This feels weird. I have anything *but* school on my mind. I see people we know. Whole families have come. But a lot of kids are still in class, and a lot of parents are still at work.

But this is good. Helpers are here. We will find Frenchie.

Then don't you know it, the folks in charge ask everyone to gather up.

"Ugh! All we do is gather up," I say. "Gather, gather, gather. Can we please start searching?" I scruff around in a circle on the school driveway.

"I know it seems that way," Pop says. "But come on, let's

listen." He hauls me in against his side, where I squirm.

"An organized effort is paramount," Mom says. She stands close to Gracia, but keeps her eye on Cedar. He is on the ground for now and wants to run. They are letting him be loose as long as they can. He'll be riding in the backpack, and it could be a while. He's not going to like that.

I let myself think it: Maybe we will find Frenchie right away.

Gracia draws in a big breath and sighs. "This waiting is very hard," she whispers. Her jaw is tight. She presses praying hands to her forehead. Not the first time I've seen her do it.

The organizers wanted her to wait for news at head-quarters. But Gracia told them no, she had to join the search for her boy, and she needed to be with her friends (us). They could reach her on her cell with news or questions. They promised to stay in touch.

"A reminder," the organizer calls, "we are working from *point last seen*. That's where we start a search for a missing person."

"Here," I whisper, pointing my finger at the ground. The guy goes on.

"We know Frenchie was dropped off at the school this morning. We believe he either left the building shortly after entering, or never entered at all. So right here, is the last place anyone saw him."

I glance at Pop. We are pretty sure he's the last one who saw Frenchie. Well, except for Cedar. Maybe. He could have been watching from our van when Frenchie walked into the school. Pop shakes his head and sighs. I think he feels the same kind of awful I feel. I bet we want the same thing: a do-over, starting from about 7:43 this morning. But he's not the one who lost Frenchie. That was me.

"We are focusing our search on the two-mile radius all around the school." The guy draws a wide loop with his finger. "Check your phone apps for the map. Images should be coming up any second now, thanks to Dottie Sylvania—our librarian and tech specialist at headquarters. She is on it! You'll see the circular area of the search cut up into pie slices." He shows us with his hands. "Each group walks a widening triangle outward from this center point—a pie slice."

"So let's go-o-o . . . ," I growl.

"Your work is to crisscross within your pie slice. Cover it all. Refer to the app to stay on track. Headquarters will keep us in the loop. In the event of changes you'll get new instructions."

"Changes? Like what?" I ask.

Pop shushes me and gestures at the speaker. "Keep listening," he says.

"What we mean is the development of a last known position. It's different from a last point seen. A last known position means Frenchie Livernois has been seen, *or* a clue

183

has been discovered that lets us know he was most likely in that location. Could be anything from a footprint to a lunch bag, to a piece of clothing. Watch as you travel. If you find anything, message headquarters immediately. A last known position, or LKP, can change the focus of our search."

I can't listen anymore. I'm ready to walk—a pie slice, a doughnut hole. Whatever. I turn in a circle looking out and think, Where would I go?

No. That's wrong thinking. The question is: Where would Frenchie go?

I think of how the sun strikes the front doors of the school on clear mornings. Frenchie lets it shine on his face before he goes inside. Did he do that this morning? If he left the school grounds, would he walk toward that sun and across Bert Gray Road? What would matter most to him?

"Okay, here it is." Mom waves the phone, then holds it low for all of us to see. "There's our triangle in the yellow highlight." She looks up. "So . . . back of the school and to the northwest. That's our slice of the pie." She smiles at Gracia. Gives her a nod.

It's good to know that we are about to actually do something.

I keep looking up because . . .

Birds.

Birds would matter to Frenchie. Birds in trees. There

are gosh-darn trees all around us.

"Okay. Stay safe out there and stay in touch. The search begins!"

"The search *resumes*," I say. "Some people have already been looking all morning."

As soon as I say it, I see one of them. Mr. Menkis. With Frenchie missing there is no one for him to watch over today. Instead, he is sitting on the curb, orange vest and backpack on, lacing his hiking boots. He sees me too. He lifts his chin at me. I wave back, but then I duck my head. What if he's wondering why I wasn't careful this morning—why I didn't bring Frenchie to him?

I watch my own feet as I follow Mom and Pop and Gracia to the back of the school, to our slice of pie—the worst kind ever—with Cedar running along beside me.

Carney Huggins

Seeing Clearly

Carney Huggins stopped at the kitchen door, two pairs of hiking boots under one arm and a couple of well-worn day packs slung on the other. He dropped all that gear and leaned on the jamb, watching his sweet Anzie at work. She was carefully sliding the remains of the smashed pies from his Punkinville Road mishap out of their tins and into her deep-dish baking pan. Carney thought she was doing an artful job of fitting the sections together, like a miniature landscape of dark purple rivers, with islands of amber-colored crusts. Odd-looking pie, but it had the look of something you'd scoop with a big spoon and feed to a crowd. Fitting.

Carney and Anzie would be heading down to the Fire

and Rec Center soon to join that search for the silent boy. When Ed and Rene Petrequin delivered the news, Anzie's double oven was hot and stacked full of half-baked pies. Excruciating choice, but they'd decided to let the pies finish while they gathered their gear. Then they'd dash out—about a half hour behind their neighbors.

"Nice repair," Carney said as Anzie used a spatula to pat a flat top on her reconstructed pastry.

"It'll do. We'll take it to headquarters with us," she said. "If the search goes long, they'll want to feed people. Or, if not, the firefighters will appreciate it. I hope we get there and learn that Frenchie's been found, safe and sound. Poor kid." She released a worried sigh. "He must be terrified," she muttered.

Carney held his bottom lip between his teeth. He managed to nod, but he was thinking that Anzie might not be right in this case. The boy called Frenchie didn't strike him as one who knew terror; the kid *was whatever he was*, wasn't he? Carney let out a nearly silent sound like *Hunh*. Who else could he say that about? And what would one call that anyway?

"Hey, Carne, clean T-shirt for you, maybe?" Anzie pointed at the evidence of spilled pies and garden mud, staining the front of Carney. "Seventeen minutes to go," she said, checking her kitchen timer.

"Yes, my beloved," he said. He peeled off his shirt at the sink and ran suds up his arms. He found the trail of blueberry stain running from his pinkie to his elbow. He scrubbed, then cupped water in his hands to wash the garden grit out of his eyes. He blinked. Twice. What Carney wanted was to see clearly. To see what had really happened earlier in the day. Then he would know. He'd be sure.

Was it a patch of plaid? Or a sparrow flying by? Could it have been the boy everyone was looking for? He shook his head. He should know the difference between a boy and a sparrow. But sometimes things flitted by so fast, and if you didn't know that you were going care about it later, you didn't take note. Should he say that he might have seen a boy following a deer—a deer that looked like it'd stepped out of a storybook? Carney used the hand towel to dry his eye sockets. He pressed hard enough that he made himself see spots.

"You know, Anz . . . I keep thinking about something," he said. "This morning was so weird."

"Why is that?" she asked, bringing their water bottles to the sink.

"Like I told you, I stopped for a deer . . ."

"Yes. You've seen deer before, haven't you?" Anzie teased.

"This one was weird. But thing is, I took a minute there. I sat in the truck," Carney continued. "You know, collecting myself and . . . stuffing my chops with your good pie. . . ."

Anzie felt flattered. She snickered.

"But, Anz, I'm not sure . . ."

"Of what, Carney?" Anzie squinted at him. "Don't be a weirdo. Tell me!"

"I might have seen something . . . and it might have been . . . *plaid*."

"Plaid?" Anzie looked nonplussed—but only for an instant. "Oh. *Plaid*? Are you saying what I think you are saying?"

"I—I think I might be."

"What? Carney! You saw him? Why didn't you say?"

"I don't know," he said thoughtfully. "I'm not sure, and I don't want to steer them wrong. But I'm starting to think I did see Frenchie this morning out on Punkinville Road."

Carney could hear Anzie's next breath catch in her windpipe.

"Pity's sake!" she hissed. She flicked off her apron and snapped it at Carney's knees. He jumped aside. "You've been sitting on vital information!" She gave him an exasperated cussing out as she shut down the fire on her double oven.

"Anz? Your pies!"

"Pies be darned, Carney! Get your shirt on. Grab that pan. We have to go!"

Aurora

Crisscrossing

In the beginning, I run ahead of Mom and Pop and Gracia, tweeting and whistling. This feels like a race to me, the most important race I will ever be in. I'm quick, crisscrossing the skinny part of our pie slice. Sticks snap and pop, and ferns brush my knees, and sometimes I have to duck under a bough, or unstick my hair from an old grabber branch.

Here in the narrow point of our pie shape, I reach the boundaries quickly. Pop is not far behind me. He looks at the map on his phone and he says, "Turn, Aurora. Turn again. That's right. Criss and cross."

At first, we can see other groups on both sides of us. Orange vests moving in and out of the trees. Then the pie slices widened, and we all spread out. The groups are going at different paces. Every so often someone calls Frenchie's name. Sometimes it's Gracia. Sometimes me. Sometimes we hear it off in the distance.

Frenchie!

Frenchie?

Cedar, riding in the pack on Pop's back echoes, "*En-chee. En-chee.*"

I realize something: I should have grabbed that megaphone back at the school and made a few announcements. I know things. I know Frenchie likes to stop and run his hands through a patch of cinnamon ferns and pat a head of Queen Anne's lace. But he doesn't like the scratchy feel of lichen-covered boulders. I know he doesn't climb trees. But if there are birds in a tree, he will stand below, looking up. Then he'll flap and tweet when they fly away. I stop still.

That's important!

It's one of the only sounds he makes. None of these searchers know that. I cup my hands around my mouth and yell.

"Hey! Everybody! Frenchie can whistle!"

There is silence. Then voices calling back, asking questions. But they are muffled by the land and the trees. If I can't hear them clearly, they didn't hear me right either.

"No!" Pop booms. "Not found! Neg-a-tive!" He makes a call on his cell right away, and I know I've done wrong.

"Aurora!" Mom comes running forward to speak to me. "You must not shout out like that. You'll confuse the searchers."

"Sorry," I say, and you can bet I'm whispering now.

"It's okay, Rene," says Gracia. "Don't scold." She tells me I am right to want the searchers to know everything that I know. "Details can help. They said so at headquarters." She's being sweet. But I want to shrink down to mini-mushroom size.

Pop pockets his phone again. "We're all set," he says. "Headquarters will message everyone, and they'll share the fact that Frenchie can whistle. The search continues," he says, and he swings his arm into the air. Cedar likes that. He copies him.

I would like to apologize one more time, and make it as loud as my blurt. But I'd be repeating a mistake. I go back to hiking, and back to what I was thinking about.

Birds. Frenchie's all about birds. A lot of birds live in trees. It's worth looking up every so often, I decide.

The sun is high and it shines down on the woods. I think I have never noticed the light and dark and light and dark of the woods—not quite this way. This is how the deer hide. How the birds blend in. I think of the day I couldn't find Cedar. The Worst Possible. I watch for khaki pants now, and a plaid shirt, and the dark berry-red of a needlepoint purse. I take a deep breath. The way it comes into my chest reminds me of reading the poem on Anzie's barn. I don't yell. I whisper.

"'SUN RAIN WIND SWEPT . . .'"

I know the rest the way Anzie wrote it. It's a poem to her farm, for everything that's true there. But what about here? What's true about now? I look around me, then change the next line.

"LEAF SHADOW SHINE . . ."

I step along to the new words. I add more.

"SWEET FERN SECRET KEPT . . ."

What else? I keep hiking.

"BOULDER BLOSSOM VINE."

I whisper the lines.

"SUN RAIN WIND SWEPT
LEAF SHADOW SHINE
SWEET FERNS SECRET KEPT
BOULDER BLOSSOM VINE."

It's a poem now. A poem I can walk to.

Jewell Laramie

Zooming In

Jewell Laramie changed all her plans for the day. She had a thing or two to take care of before she could join the search. But join she would. First, she went home and sent out a message postponing the softball league picnic. She added a note about the missing boy and requested that all "fit and able" folks lend themselves to the search. Then she packed her Jeep—almost the way she had planned for earlier in the day, but now her purpose had changed.

She was back at the Fire and Rec Center filling the big fridge with the hot dogs and salads she'd purchased for the softball league picnic. Those would be supper for the searchers now. The garden club had offered to cook and serve. She backed her head out of the fridge as Carney Huggins and Anzie Mayfield arrived with a pan of deep-dish pie. Blueberry, from the purple looks of it. To be helpful, Jewell went to take the pan from Anzie. That put her close enough to hear Carney telling Chief Nash about a deer having jumped in front of his truck on Punkinville Road earlier that morning.

Jewell turned with the pan, and on her way to the fridge and thought, Well, didn't that happen all the time? Deer in the road? This was Maine. And why had Carney Huggins chosen this moment to tell a deer story, anyway? What did it have to do with the search? She stowed the pie quickly and came back to eavesdrop.

She heard Carney say something about buckets rolling in the road. Then she saw Anzie give her fella a good knuckle to the arm. "Tell them the rest, Carne!"

Then Carney told about a possible—but not definite—flash of plaid. Jewell's ears perked up at that. She'd seen it written on the whiteboard: Frenchie Livernois, was last seen wearing a plaid shirt.

Those in charge checked the large map on a big screen that librarian Dottie Sylvania had set up special for the search. They discussed terrain, saying moderate to easy in terms of hiking. They estimated the distance and looked at the time.

"Seems unlikely," Chief Nash said. "The boy started the morning here." He moved the cursor along the map and stopped at Mountain View School near the top of Bert Gray Road. "How would he make it to Punkinville Road? And what? Fly up over a fifty-foot rock face here at the preserve?"

"North," Jewell heard Carney say, though he was talking behind one hand, in a sort of thinking pose. "It happened closer to here," he said, and he tapped the screen with his finger.

"That's still a lot of open land to cross and it—"

"Flattens out," Jewell interjected. "Much more level overall if you're crossing farther north." With all eyes on her now, she added, "Ask any deer. Ask any hunter." She worked her eyebrows up and down. She turned to Carney. "You say you saw a boy and a deer. It could be they're using the same trail."

"Wait. Are you saying this boy and a deer are traveling together?" Chief Nash squinted at Jewell.

"No!" Jewell said. "I am saying my fellow sporting folks and I have tracked deer for miles, using their paths. I'm saying walking a trail, even an animal trail, is easier than bushwhacking." She elbowed her way up to the large screen, Dottie shifting quickly to let her in. "Carney, come take a look at this with me."

Jewell traced her finger along the screen.

"There's a known deer trail about here. Weaves down from upper Bert Gray Road like so. Not far from the school," Jewell noted. "Heading west to east, the trail crosses Punkinville Road right about here." She looked at Carney. "Yes?"

"That's the place. Roughly," said Carney.

"The hiking would be easy enough for a healthy, woodsy kiddo," Jewell said. "There are several deer 'bedrooms,' along the trail and one ends here." She drew a circle with her finger. "Just southeast of where you were."

"Hmm," said Carney Huggins. He cupped his chin in his hand and closed one eye at the map on the screen.

"What?" Anzie said. "Carney, say what's on your mind."

"Hmm ... direction," he said. "Both the deer and the boy—if it was a boy at all—they came from the other side of the road. Both were traveling east to west."

Jewell closed herself off from the ensuing chatter. She did not like the idea of getting steered off a solid lead. There was a vulnerable boy out there, and he needed to be found. She helped herself to the cursor and manipulated the map to reveal a plot of land deeper to the east, closer to the river, and not so far from the seashore. She switched the aerial view and zoomed in on the broccoli-like tops of trees, and the pale trapezoid of a farm field. Closer, closer. Ah! She found what she was looking for.

"Yo," said Jewell. "I say, yo!" Everyone huddled behind her. She traced a faint line that cut across the corner of the field. "This is trampled earth, as seen from above," she said. "It's the deer path, and see, it disappears into the woods here." She pointed out what looked like a small dark, depression in the landscape.

"See that?" she said. "Slight clearing. The path ends here. Because, if they kept going, the deer would reach the seashore before too long, and I don't need to tell you, deer prefer the woods, meadows, and barrens. So what they do here is they rest." Her eyes were on the screen now, and Jewell was trancelike in her belief that this was an area of interest. "This is a deer 'bedroom.' They'll stay here, usually all day, but not always. Then, like most creatures when they reach the end of a trail, they turn around and head back." She took a breath. "That, my friends, could explain why the boy was heading east to west."

Aurora

Last Known Position

"Hold up!" Pop calls.

We have been out for over an hour when the message comes in.

"There's news?" Gracia asks, and her voice pipes with hope.

I hold my breath and do not blurt, but I am wishing, wishing, wishing.

Have they found him? Is Frenchie all right?

But the news isn't quite that good.

"They're bringing us in," Pop says.

"What?"

"Yep." He wipes his forehead with his bandanna.

"There's an LKP—last known position. Apparently, some-body saw Frenchie late this morning." Pop smiles like it's good news, and Gracia takes a big breath in and grabs Mom's arm.

"Really? Where?" she asks.

"Punkinville Road," says Pop, and Mom and Gracia fall together in a hug.

"Punkinville? Huh. So now what?" I say.

"I imagine we start over again inside a new two-mile radius," says Mom. She grunts a little as they transfer Cedar from Pop's shoulders to hers.

"So we go back to the school now?"

"That's right," says Pop. "Then to headquarters at the Fire and Rec Center for our new assignment."

I am wilting inside, but I try not to show it. This feels wrong. I feel pulled, like I want to keep walking the way we were going. I don't want to leave our slice of lost-person pie unsearched. It's hard not to feel as if we have walked this far for nothing, and now it's going to take us almost as long to get back, except we won't bother to crisscross. We will walk a straight line. Then I remember something from math class: the shortest path from point A to point B is always a straight line.

Mom and Pop and Gracia are already on the march, heading back to the school, and I know I have to go with them.

I look over my shoulder, and call out one more time,

"Frenchie! Frenchie?" Then I whisper, "Coming to get you, wherever you are."

A straight line *is* a lot shorter. I am surprised when we step back onto the playing field and see the school. Everything looks a little weird. This is not the way we come to school. I wonder if the day is going on like normal, except for me, out here searching, and Darleen Dombroski, who is out here somewhere having her lesson.

We hustle in to use the bathrooms. Cedar gets a fresh diaper, and Mom gives him a belly buzz and a good-egg award. He's ridden a long way in the pack today. Mom sets him on his feet and lets him run up and down the halls of school. He's laughing his curly head off. I crack a big grin, and take a run with him. He rounds the corner, and I hurry to grab him before he reaches the classrooms and I hear my name.

"Aurora!" I turn.

"Leena! Joanie!" I am so happy to see them. They come running up to hug me.

"We have been so worried about you," Joanie says.

"About me?"

"Yes. Because Frenchie is your friend, and this is scary," Leena says. I feel my next swallow go down hard.

"I'm fine but so worried about Frenchie," I say.

"We are too. Everyone is. The ever-changing tree mural is full of notes for him." Leena smiles. I know she wants me to feel better. "If the notes were leaves, you could rake them into a pile and jump in!"

"Saw that." I nod. "Even before I left school this morning there were lots of them."

I tell them about the search—quickly. I think to myself:

SUN RAIN WIND SWEPT
LEAF SHADOW SHINE
SWEET FERNS SECRET KEPT
BOULDER BLOSSOM VINE.

"They want us to move to a new area," I tell my friends. "Somebody thinks they saw him."

"Oh, that's good! So good!" Joanie gives my arm a pump. Then Cedar comes running and bashes into all three of us and wraps our knees in his arms.

"Ugh!" We almost fall over. Joanie and Leena laugh and cuddle Cedar.

"Are you helping?" Leena asked him, and he nods. "You're searching for Frenchie?"

"Yeah. En-chee," says Cedar. "Bye-baw, bye-baw."

"What's that?" Leena asks.

"No idea," I say with a shrug.

"Hey, I better go catch up to my family. Frenchie's mom is with us," I add.

"I wish I could come with you, Aurora." Joanie frowns. Her shoulders drop.

"We hope our parents will let us help after school," says Leena. "But my mom's working on the food truck straight into suppertime."

Suppertime. Wow. I think about all the walking we have done and wonder if they'll still assign search areas (pie slices) so late in the day. For the first time I think about how the sun will go down. I try to remember what time that happens now that the days have grown shorter. I think of the chilly evenings.

We have got to find Frenchie.

I take Cedar's hand to leave, and Joanie says, "Hey, Aurora. we still want to know what you were going to tell us. Your story."

"What story?"

"About your geode. You were about to tell us this morning. But Mr. Menkis came in, and then Ms. Beccia started class. And then . . . well . . ."

"Oh. Right," I say. I reach into my pocket and curl my fingers around my half of the geode. "It can wait," I tell them.

Outside in the parking lot volunteers are handing out apples, bananas, and energy bars to the searchers as they come out of the woods and back across Bert Gray Road.

I see Darleen Dombrowski. She has one shoe off and she's leaning against the water truck. Her mother is dabbing Darleen's ankle with damp paper towels. Looks like she got scraped up out on the trail. She wipes her eyes, and her lip quivers. I know that an ankle-skinning can sting like heck. I feel bad for snapping at her when she said searching for Frenchie would be a good lesson—not that it doesn't still grind my insides. But now she is sniffling and miserable. I actually think it: Poor Darleen.

"Ah! Fuel!" Pop says, eyeing the snacks.

"Take one of everything," a lady tells him. "There's plenty, and you're all working so hard out there. You'll need calories to find that boy. Then go see Charlie and Edna to get your water bottles filled. Tank is right there on their pickup."

Pop thanks her and calls me over.

"Aurora. Come grab a bite."

"Or two or three!" the lady says. She holds up apples in both hands.

I shrug. Pop motions to me—being pushy this time. I shrug again. But when I see that probably every searcher is choosing a snack too, including Mom and Gracia, I take an energy bar and an apple.

"How about you, Cedar Tree? Hungry?"

He's not shy. He grabs two bars.

We get into the car and roll out of the lot.

"Oh, food!" Mom says.

"I'm not sure I can eat," says Gracia. "Maybe a nibble."

I am not sure I can eat anything either. I've felt a hollow in me all day. Every so often it fills up with worry. I make myself bite into the apple. It is crisp and sweet. Suddenly, I can hardly cram it in fast enough. It's like the lady said: calories. Calories for finding Frenchie. Cedar polishes off both of his energy bars and grabs at my apple core. Mom gives him a banana. Gracia's eating one too. She takes small bites and deep breaths.

"I feel like we are going to find him now," she says.

I look out the window. It's so weird. I've got no proof. I've got no reason at all, but I still feel like we're headed in the wrong direction.

Frenchie

Eat Sleep

Frenchie marched in under the trees right behind the piebald deer. Half a dozen more deer popped their heads up out of the ferns.

Plain deer. No spots.

They looked at Frenchie with their dark eyes. He heard a snort, then saw all the white tails flip up as they ran away.

The piebald deer looked as if it might go with them. But it stayed. It ate green leaves. Frenchie ate the sandwich from his backpack.

Soon the piebald deer settled in one of the lie-down places the other deer had left behind. Frenchie chose one too. He rested and listened.

He heard birds.

Insects.

People.

Someone said his name.

Frenchie stayed low and quiet. The piebald deer had closed its triangle-patch eyes. It was sleeping.

Quiet is for sleeping.

Aurora

Seeing Home

I have Pop's phone in the back seat of the van. I'm looking at where we have been. There's the search circle with the school as the center point, and all the slices of the pie, including ours. I can see the path we took and where we stopped when we got word to come back in.

"See anything yet, Aurora?" Pop asks.

"Nope," I say. I'm watching for a new circle to come up on the screen.

"Oh, I hope it's not a glitch. We don't need that." Gracia sighs.

"Well, Mrs. Sylvania is a technology supergenius," I say. "She's probably working on it right now." I look at the screen, and a new circle appears on the map right before my eyes.

"Ha! Hey, you guys," I say, "here it is! The new circle overlaps the first one. Looks like a Venn diagram. You know, with stuff in common in the middle?" If Frenchie were not missing, I might love all of this.

"Ahh . . . ," says Gracia. "That's why they wanted the searchers on the east side of Bert Gray Road to stay on the job and finish hiking their pie slices. That area falls inside Aurora's Venn diagram."

I don't know how Gracia can do it on this awful day, but she gives me a smile.

"That makes sense," says Pop.

I still have the phone. I study the new circle. Then I shout.

"HOME!"

They all gasp. Pop taps the break and the van lurches.

"Good grief, Aurora!" he says. "I thought I was about to hit something!"

Outbursts are worse inside a car.

"Sorry, so sorry," I say. "But you have to see this! The new search includes *home*. Look, look. Bottom of the circle." I pass the phone up to Gracia. Mom turns in the front seat and they share. Pop keeps his eyes on the road.

"Aurora is right," Gracia says.

"Sure is," says Mom. "So . . . the new center point is

partway up Punkinville. That must be where someone saw Frenchie."

Thinks they saw him. I keep it to myself. I am wondering lots of things, but one of the biggest ones is this: If Frenchie was that close to home, why didn't he go home? He always knows the way.

Gracia keeps looking at the new search circle. "All of Flanders Pond is included, then the edge of the circle taps the southern part of Lake Road and sweeps just south enough to include our houses, and Baker Hill and Tucker Mountain."

"He's been to all those places before," I say, but I am quiet about it. "We all have. We've hiked them together."

By the time we reach the meetup on Punkinville Road, a message has come in. Mom has the phone now. She reads, then tells us, "No pie slices this time. They are focusing on areas. This is good," she says. "The Pond Association is activating a search all around their shores and beyond. A hiking club is covering Tucker Mountain. We're to focus on a network of deer trails."

"Near home?" I ask.

"Not really." She shakes her head. "North of home, heading west to Bert Gray. Back to the school."

"So, wait a minute. Frenchie started at the school, cut all the way over to Punkinville Road, and now they think he's going back to the school? Sheesh! Why didn't we stay there? We weren't done searching our pie slice!" I

bounce my head against the seat back—several times—
and think:

SUN RAIN WIND SWEPT
DARN IT DARN IT DARN IT

There is nothing to do but follow directions. That's
how you can be the most helpful. Mom and Pop and Gracia have said it again and again. We go where they send
us, and begin to walk a narrow path on the west side of
Punkinville Road.

Sometimes it seems like the trail has ended or tapers
down so thin, or opens up so broad, we aren't sure we are
on it anymore. It's a little nutty to say, but we are following the path we see on the phone, even when it doesn't
seem like the ground is doing the right thing.

Sometimes we meet up with other groups. Crossing a
stretch of meadow, Jewell Laramie spots me.

"Aurora P.!" she calls. "Oh! And all the Ps!" She plows
through the grass, smashing down the goldenrod on her
way. When she realizes that Gracia is with us too, she hugs
her extra tight. "I'm so sorry. I know this must be excruciating."

"Thank you," Gracia says. "I am grateful to everyone
for helping us search for my son. Please tell others I said
so, will you?"

"Of course. And listen, we will not stop," Jewell says.

211

The grown-ups talk and sip water.

I march in place. I'm an object in motion, and I'm going to stay in motion.

When Jewell asks me how I am doing, I tell her. "I won't be all right until Frenchie is found."

"I'm with ya, kiddo." She offers me a knuckle bump. When we touch, she wraps her other hand tight around both our fists. I have to smile. Otherwise I don't think she'll give me back my hand. She says, "If Carney Huggins is right abou—"

"Carney Huggins?" I blurt.

"Yut. Carney's the one who spotted Frenchie on Punkinville."

"You don't say?" says Pop. "News to us."

"All we heard was *somebody*," Mom says. "We know Carney, and of course we know Anzie, very well."

"Yut," says Jewell. "If you ask me, he had some useful information—and all because of a near miss! Whew!" She leans back on her heels.

"A near miss?" Gracia tilts her head at Jewell.

"He stopped for a deer in the road. That's when he saw a flash of plaid. You know, just happened that they were all in the same place at the same time. But it sure got me thinking that it makes all sorts of sense that Frenchie is walking these deer trails," says Jewell.

"I don't get it. Why do you say so?" I want to know.

Jewell stoops down low, eye level with the tops of the

grasses. "Easy passages," she says. "Look at that. That's a kiddo-shaped space if I ever did see one. A path is a sweet discovery. It's already there for us, so we take it. Don't you think?"

I shrug. "I kind of like climbing over stuff," I say.

Jewell laughs out loud. She says, "I guess you do, Aurora P. Always honest!"

Jewell leaves us—to do some retracing and recalculating, she says. It's late afternoon, the sun shines like a little fire on my forehead. I look left and right. I swish the grasses with my hands on both sides of the trail and look in, as if I might see Frenchie curled up in a ground nest. Waiting for us.

Mom and Pop let Cedar get down again. He runs up the trail. I pass everyone to stay close behind him.

"If he ducks into the grass, we could lose him!" I shout.

But then I see that Cedar takes the path. Only the path. Because it's already there for him, like Jewell said.

Maxine Grindel

Upon Waking

Maxine Grindel opened her eyes. She was sitting in a chair at her front window. Same spot she'd been since late morning when she and Dudley had returned from the emergency clinic. Same old view of Bert Gray Road between the trunks of the tall pines. Her orange cat was resting on her lap, and in turn, Maxine rested her wrapped finger on the cat's ample back. Dudley had kept her apprised, between her many unintentional naps that day, about the search for the missing boy.

"Any more news?" she asked groggily. "Are they still up at the . . . ooo-ahhh . . . sssch . . . coool?" She lost that sentence in an enormous yawn, but Dudley understood her.

"Believe so," he said.

"Oh, me . . . wish we could be out there helping," Maxine sighed. "Did I tell you, I've met that boy? Charmed me into a Mrs. Thrift deep discount on a pretty-pretty needlepoint purse without speaking a word. Hmm . . . Did I tell you that, Dudley?"

"You did. A dozen times, darlin'."

"Oh no, I did not!" Maxine protested.

"You did. It's fine."

"Well, it's breaking my heart," she said. "I want to join that search."

"Me too," said Dudley. "But we need to tend to you today."

Maxine knew that her immediate future was all about sleeping off that wild medication and taking care of her finger. She was going to miss the flea market in Searsport the next morning anyway. "Mrs. Thrift takes a sales hit," she mumbled. "Doctor's orders." She glanced at her bandaged finger, a.k.a. Miss Mummy. "Piddling," Maxine said, because nothing was more important than finding that boy—oh, his poor mother, and his poor little loud friend. She must ache for him. Mrs. Thrift knew a special bond when she saw one.

Soon, the purring of her cat and the sunshine beaming in the window between the tall pines combined forces and sent Maxine back to napping. But not for as long this time.

When she woke, Dudley was bringing tea and crackers for her, and a late lunch with an early beer for himself. Maxine thanked her fella. She took a slow steamy sip, and oh, that tea tasted good. A few sips later, she felt like she might finally be coming back to life. She looked out at her busted lawn chair. She vaguely recalled having taken a hard landing on it. Oh, in fact and she'd gone *through* it. Right. She was fainting at the time. The webbing had not held.

Heavens! Was she ever going to regain her handle on this day? The crumpled chair frame and torn webbing still lay on the carpet of pine needles that spread right out to the edge of the road—and the road, Maxine noticed, seemed busy now.

"Lot of traffic. Looks like it could be coming down from the school," she said.

"Maybe they're on the move," Dudley said. He took a look at his phone.

"Think it means he's been found?"

"Naw . . . I think Charlie and Edna would have sent a message in that case. They're up there. Took a tank of drinking water in the back on of their truck. But you're right, Maxie. That is a lot of cars."

"Curious," Maxine said. She suddenly felt bored and thought she might like to get up. She shifted under the weight of the cat and got back an offended look. She purred at him, and he settled again. He was a sweet cat—when he wasn't sneaking outside to taunt the back-yard birds.

Oh, the birds.

"Dudley," Maxine asked, "did you remember to fill the feeder?"

"Oh. I remember now," he said.

"Well, you know what? I want to do it," she told him.

"Oh, Maxie, are you sure?" Dudley did not put down his sandwich.

"Yes," she said, and she eased herself out from under the cat. She waggled Miss Mummy at Dudley.

"I think *we* can handle the task," she joked, and Dudley laughed with his mouth full. "We'll holler if we need you."

"I'll listen for you," he said. "Steady now, darling."

Maxine did feel steady. She stepped into her slippers (no laces to tie), and made her way to the kitchen pantry. She protected her injured finger and scooped a pitcher full of sunflower seeds, one-handed. She popped the latch on the back door with her elbow and swung it open. She stopped on the step and took in a deep breath of the warm September afternoon. Ahh! This was just what she needed.

She glanced into the yard. There was a *spotted* animal standing at her birdfeeder. She opened her eyes wider than she had all day. Maxine blinked. Twice.

What a strange jewel of a creature—oh, a deer! *Was it*

a deer? Since when did deer wear patches of all those colors—chestnut and chocolate, snowy white, and roan red. It looks *quilted*! Maxine thought.

She stood stock-still. She watched the deer give the feeder a good nudge with its black bulbous nose. With its pretty-pretty lips, it swept the last of the sunflower seed out of the lowest feeder hole.

"Dudley . . . ," Maxine whispered, though not loud enough to be heard. What to do? He *must* come see this. Maxine was in a pickle; if she went to get Dudley the deer might well be gone by the time they came back. If she called for him too loudly the animal would scare.

Maxine stayed stuck for several long minutes. If only she had been able to take her eyes off that magnificent deer, she might have seen the boy in the plaid shirt and khaki pants. He was standing with one cheek pressed against the smooth gray trunk of a beech tree, no more than thirty feet away from Maxine and her back door.

Frenchie

The Cool Tree

The tree trunk felt cool on Frenchie's cheek. It smelled good too. Outdoor things often did smell good. The deer was eating seeds like birds eat seeds. Frenchie could hear the cars going by on the road. Not far.

Cars are not a good time to cross.

But Frenchie thought the deer would cross like it had in the morning because it was going back now. He remembered:

Let's follow. For as long as it'll let us.

He was still thinking that Aurora would come. The school was close again, and Frenchie knew the way.

He heard a latch click and a person came out the door. Slippers on the feet. Not shoes. She was Mrs. Thrift.

Frenchie squeezed the needlepoint purse against his side. Mrs. Thrift had lots of things. She might have more seeds for the deer. But she didn't come off the step.

She stood as still as a cool tree.

Aurora

Just Over a Year Ago;
Ezelda Trink's Quarry

This search for Frenchie is taking us over all sorts of Maine terrain. We scuff through the gray dust and peastone beside a gravel pit, and it makes me think of the day we visited the quarry.

Mom had a story to write about an artist who owned a quarry. Or part of one. Inactive, is what Mom told me. Except, hey, a quarry means a whole lot of rock. And trees and water mean a whole lot of birds. *And* the place was open to the public. I knew it probably wasn't the place to find a nice tourmaline specimen, but it sounded cool, and it wasn't far from home.

"Close as the crow flies," Pop said. He says that about

a lot of places, because our roads do wind the long way around.

We took a picnic on a hot day last summer. Frenchie and Gracia came with us. We packed a cooler because mom was scared our sandwiches would turn putrid before we got to eating them.

We followed the signs up a loopy road that turned to dirt and parked our van in a scrubby, sloped lot. Pop and I had to drag the cooler up a path. At the top were giant pieces of granite sunk into the ground all in a row—all of them taller than Pop. We wedged our way between them.

"Sheesh!" I said. "Good thing we're not hauling a double-wide, Pop. Good thing we don't mind banging up our cooler and scraping off our hip bones."

"I'll say! Phew!" Pop sat down hard on the cooler and fanned himself with his hat. Mom let Cedar slide off her hip. She took a few photos and scribbled some notes while Gracia took a brochure out of a box on a post. Frenchie and I walked a few more feet. We stood shoulder to shoulder looking over the place.

"Whoa!" I said. "It's like a rock fun park! Cut right into the earth. Mom! You should put that in the story!" There were pools of black and green water, and clusters of lily pads with pink star-shaped blooms sitting on top, and purple pickerel weed. Plants grew up out of cracks in the gray rocks. There were granite sculptures everywhere, carved with suns, swirls, whales, and fish. There was a bank of heaped-up, jagged rocks—all sizes—from the quarry's old working days. I knew because I'd seen photos of the mines in Androscoggin.

Way out across a big pool of dark water, I could see a tall gray wall of granite, the highest side of the quarry. It was at least as high as the peak of our A-frame.

"Mom! Pop! Did you know it would be like this?" I called to them. "How come we've never been here before?"

"Welcome!" There came a woman with a crinkly smile, her gray hair in a floppy bun. She had on a heavy apron and spatters of clay had dried on her arms. "I take it you are the writer?" she said to Mom. "I see you found the brochure. Map is on the flipside. Do you have any questions?"

"I do!" I said. "How'd those monster stones get there? I mean, right in the way and all?" I jabbed my thumb over my shoulder at the tall standing rocks.

"Those are my megaliths," she said. "Took me a whole summer working with Gorgeous, sun up to sun down to plant them. Had some help from my friends to set them upright into the holes and backfill."

"Wait, wait. Working with Gorgeous? Who's he?"

"She! Gorgeous is my backhoe. She's rusty, trusty, and good."

"And what about you?"

"I'm rusty, trusty, and not as good."

"No! I mean what's your name?"

"Ezelda Trink. Welcome to my quarry."

"Ee-zelda Trink," I repeated. "And this is your own quarry. Wow. So do you want to be called Ms. or Mrs. Trink?" I asked.

"Call me Ezelda."

"Okay. So Ee-zelda, about those *megaliths*, did you ever think people might want to drive their cars right up to the top here?" I asked.

"That's exactly what I thought," she said. "But I wanted to keep cars down there, and artistry and natural beauty up here." She stretched her arms wide.

I gave my sweaty head a scratch. I looked at Mom and Pop and Gracia. They were going to let me handle this. "Well, what about wheelchair access? Ever think of that?"

"Did. That's when I call up to the house for Gary. He's an artist in residence. Came for two months and stayed for two years." She chuckled. "We go down together and help anyone who needs us—if they need us, that is. It's an incline, after all, not a ski slope. Wheelchairs and baby strollers fit between the megaliths. Gorgeous and I made sure of that."

She shut one eye at me. "You're a thoughtful girl," she said.

"Oh. Thanks. A lot of people say I'm annoying."

Ezelda the artist snorted. "Unimaginable," she said.

She smiled a gentle kind of smile at Frenchie. "Quiet soul," she said. She looked at the three parents. Maybe wondering who he belonged to.

"He's a *silent soul*," I said. "Well, maybe not." I looked right at Gracia. She smiled and nodded. "What I mean is, he doesn't talk with words. So you have to *look* for his answers."

"Makes things interesting for you, then, doesn't it?" Ezelda said.

"Yeah." I shrugged. "But I get him. Like right now, he looks like he's having a big old stare at nothing. But he's really looking for birds. They're his favorite. He's birds. I'm rocks. Hey, mind if I do some rock hunting here? On your property?"

"That's fine. As long as rocks is all you're hunting. After anything in particular?"

"Tourmaline," I said. "I'm always after tourmaline. It's here. I mean, probably not right here. But it is in Maine. In case you didn't know. One of these days I'm going to visit a mine and find a vein." I sighed. I looked all around her place. "But thanks for letting me look. Oh, and if I do find it, can I keep it?"

"You're welcome to take all the stone you can carry."

Well, that was all I needed to forget all about lunch. I was off. Except Mom grabbed the tail of my T-shirt before I got away. I kept marching. I made windmill arms.

"Ah, Aurora, let's please take a look at Ezelda's map first."

"And a few safety rules," Gracia added.

The quarry had parts. Right close was the picnic area and a wading pool. A short walk across some flat rock and there was a shallow swimming pond.

"The most important note," Ezelda said, "is that there's no admittance beyond the fence. You see?" She pointed to a split rail that circled a huge, watery hole surrounded by the high wall of granite. "That's a deep-water quarry. Cold as can be, and not safe."

"Got it," I said.

"Best way to view it is through these." She flipped open the lid on a wooden box attached to a post and pulled out an old set of binoculars. "You'll find more binocular boxes on the property. Maybe your birder will enjoy them."

I put them right up to my eyes and scanned all around the quarry.

"What's that hill full of crunchy-looking stone?"

"Grout," she said. "It's scrap from the mining days. Jagged cast-offs. I banked it up with help from Gorgeous. Another deterrent for those who ignore fences and think they want to go dip in the deep water. I can't have that."

"Oh . . . I see," I said.

I was still looking through the binoculars, imagining the old quarrying days, and looking at the stripes in the granite, and the way plants had taken root in the stone. I already knew that granite was superhard igneous rock with mica, quartz, and feldspar in it. Some of the crystals were catching the sun. I traced my way up the farthest and highest part of the quarry wall, all the way to the top.

"Hey!" I said. "P-people up there! Right now! You said no hiking allowed up on that ledge."

"I don't allow them," Ezelda grumbled. "They ride their ATVs and motorbikes in from the town parcel, and completely ignore the property markers. They've tamped a path up there, wide as a logging road. But there is little I can do." She sighed.

"Back to work with me," she said. "I'll be off this way, in the clay studio." She waved her muddy arm. "Drop in and visit. Enjoy the place!"

Well, I didn't find a piece of tourmaline that day. But Mom got her story, and I sure did like the shallow ponds of Ezelda Trink's quarry. Frenchie and I floated there, and Cedar sat splashing in the puddles with Pop. I thought about what it must have been like years ago when they cut and dragged giant slabs of granite out.

"Huh. That's kind of destructive, taking rock out of the earth like that, isn't it? Look how it's all scarred up. . . ."

Frenchie couldn't hear me that day; his ears were underwater.

Now here we are searching for him, passing by this gravel pit—and talk about scarred up. It's a funny thing, both this pit and the quarry are for harvesting stone. But the quarry is beautiful, and I'd call this gravel pit ugly. Ghost gray. Dry and weedy. But as we walk out, I remember something Ezelda Trink said. Something that I liked, because I could see it with my own eyes.

Nature has been taking back the quarry—growing it over and healing it up.

That's what I want—to get healed up. We are not finding Frenchie, and now every step leaves me with a fresh hollow in my gut.

Aurora

Trespass Trail

The land turns woodsy again. The air is cooler under the trees. The brush and boulders are taller than we are, and wider than a six-person hug. Ferns and reindeer lichens cling to them like wild heads of hair. I would love to climb them—if everything about today were different, that is. Frenchie would stay below. He doesn't like lichens. Too rough—like a tag in the neck of a shirt, I guess.

I ask for a turn carrying Cedar in the backpack. He's heavy as rocks and thinks this is a game. He pulls my hair and puts his fingers over my eyes; he bounces and hollers, "Goh! Awoh-wah! Goh!"

We walk a sponge of reddish-brown pine needles now. We step over roots. We kick up pine cones, hard little green ones and big open brown ones. My legs feel like rubber. I teeter one time too many for Mom. She takes my brother off my back.

When we reach a yard, or a clearing, it can seem like the trail has ended. And maybe it has. But headquarters drops new pins on the GPS that have us winding toward Bert Gray Road—back to the school—so we keep going.

All day long we have not really known whose land we were on. When we do see people, we explain why we are trespassing.

Gracia tells them, "My son is lost. Have you seen a young boy come through? Eleven years old."

We hand them the photocopy of his school picture. (I tell them his hair is longer now.)

Some say, "Oh! Heard about that. Went missing, huh? So sorry. Terrible thing." People promise to keep an eye out for him. They invite us to fill our water bottles. Everyone is kind.

But nobody—nobody—has seen Frenchie.

Frenchie

The High Place

The trail stopped in a high place. Frenchie stood on the edge looking out.

All rock.

He knew this place. From over there. Across. In the low.

Aurora liked all this rock. She liked the deer too, so he followed it all day long. But she had not caught up, and now Frenchie couldn't see the deer, but that might be it, making swishing sounds off in the green leaves.

A loud, dark bird made him look up. He had some loud birds in the needlepoint purse. But not this one. There was light and dark and shine, and light and dark and shine up there.

Then the bird flew out. "Caw-caw!" Black wings tilted into the blue.

Frenchie stared.

Nothing holds birds up.

Nothing keeps them up.

Now the bird was gone, so Frenchie flapped and tweeted. The needlepoint purse swung at his side. The ground under his heels made sounds. Then it broke into crumbs. Slow. Fast. Smash! His teeth clanked together. He was on his butt.

Sliding.

The high place let go of Frenchie. The branch caught him. Let him go. The rocks caught him. Let him go. He grabbed. But everything let him go.

Frenchie could not stay up on nothing.

Ezelda Trink

Things Fall

Most days, by three in the afternoon, Ezelda Trink was done working in her pottery studio. That's when she could be found—or, not found, as she preferred—leaning on the split rail fence, gazing over the deep-water quarry, and coddling a mug of good Earl Grey tea.

But this Friday afternoon harbored a rotten surprise for the artist.

She trimmed her last pot of the day from the wheel and nestled it under the long sheet of plastic at her front table with the rest of the day's successful turnings. She scrubbed her hands and toweled them dry. She turned from the sink, and when she did, she caught the loop of her apron tie on . . . something.

That something was the corner of the tall drying shelf, where a dozen pots sat ready for the kiln. Darned if Ezelda and her apron tie didn't pull the whole setup off its supports. The shelves and the clay pots came down with a crash.

Ezelda spent the next hour softly cussing to herself, and picking up shards of leather-hard pottery and tossing them into a vat of water. It was a lot of lost work at the potter's wheel. But the pieces were unfired, so they'd absorb the water and become soft clay again.

So it went. . . .

And so it was that Ezelda was *not* peacefully sipping tea in full view of the deep-water quarry at three o'clock that afternoon when Frenchie Livernois took his dreadful fall. She did *not* see him tumbling down the granite ledges, losing his belongings as he went. She neither saw nor heard the splash he made as he hit the dark cold water.

Frenchie

Right After the Fall

Frenchie's butt was killing him. Lots of stones on that slide down. And plants. Everything he'd grabbed had let him go.

The way down had taken his shoes. A branch had taken his purse with his birds inside. Now he was under the dark water. In a place of no breathing. Cold was filling his clothes, and the spaces between his toes. It seeped into the tunnels of his ears and ached there.

Above, he saw the September sun. A shiny blur.

SUN SUN SUN.

He would like to go up. But his pants were caught by one cuff on something below.

Frenchie reached down and tugged. Tried again.

Raked his finger across some hurting thing. A bubble went up. He wanted to follow it. With cold fingers he worked his belt back through the buckle. He popped the snap. Pushed the zipper down. His pants let him go. Up. Toward that sun. He burst into the breathing place.

He lay his body on the top of the water.

That's it, Frenchie! Relax and breathe.

SUN SUN SUN.

Frenchie

The Small Flat Place

Frenchie floated, and while he floated, he looked through his half-open eyes. The sun was still shining. A few birds flew by in the space between Frenchie and the sun. He was on the wrong side for seeing feather shine. The birds went like dark flickers. Like shadows, but not shadows.

The cold was taking the ache out of his backside, but it was putting an ache at his temples. He flipped over in the water. He paddled and kicked to where the rock had a spot for him. Right below where he had come down. He pulled himself onto the sun-warmed ledge.

It was a flat place.

Like a front step.

But no house and no door. There wasn't much room. Only enough for Frenchie, one tiny tree, and a patch of pale green lichen, which he wished was not there. Too scratchy. Too peely.

Aurora

Bringing Folks In

The sky has that look that reminds me of all the times I have been late for supper. Of course, it's September and the days are shorter. I already get it: headquarters will want to pull us off the search before dark. Secret decision: I won't go. Not until we find Frenchie.

At six thirty Pop gets the message.

"They are bringing folks in," he says, and the news falls hard on all of us.

Gracia gives a nod—like, trying to be brave. She and Mom hug each other. They cry a little. They whisper on each other's shoulders, then wipe their faces. Cedar leans around from the pack on Mom's back, asking, "'Kay, Mam? 'Kay?"

No. Not okay, Cedar Tree. Not.

We use this time to rest, all of us lined up on a log. Pop stares at his boots. Mom is hunched; Gracia looks like she is studying her palms. Even Cedar is silent.

I hear Gracia breath in, then out. "Well, I'm going to stay strong for my son." She stands up and looks at Pop. "Okay, Ed. What's the plan? What do they say?"

"We finish out this way," he says. He stands and points us in the direction that we've been traveling. "We're close to Bert Gray Road. Should come out not far from the school. They'll have a bus waiting to take us all back to Fire and Rec for some supper. Then to our cars from there. We'll start again in the morning."

"Not me," I say. "I'm not stopping. We don't have Frenchie."

"Aurora . . ." Mom cups her hand on the back of my head. "Another hour and it'll be too dark to see—"

"Uh-uh. Our eyes will adjust," I say. "The dark is only dark if you've been looking at light. You just have to stay out in it. Keep your pupils dilated."

"Well, I'm not sure about your theory, but . . ."

"I'm not getting on that bus. I'm going back to that land behind the school. It's a feeling I have. A feeling about Frenchie."

There, I said it. I ball up my fists and add, "I can't stop searching."

"Oh, we won't stop. But we need to make sure we are

240

at our best," Gracia says softly. She comes to me and cups her hand around one of my fists. "We need food and rest for our bodies. And sleep for our brains." She strokes my hand until my fist uncurls. Then she holds my open palm like it's the middle of a sandwich and her hands are the bread. Her eyes pool. "We need to dream our best dreams about Frenchie. And tomorrow morning, we'll begin to search again. Okay, Aurora?"

Cedar echoes. "'Kay, Awoh-wah? 'Kay?"

"Please?" Gracia says. Her tears spill.

I cannot say no to her.

Pop thinks we have a half hour to go. We walk on. Cedar starts crying, like he's doing it for all of us. I look around for something to give him—maybe a pine cone, which he'd probably love to throw at me. Instead, I find a stick with a foot-long piece of old-man's beard hanging from it. I hand it up to Cedar—on Pop's back now. It makes him so happy, he hums! He reaches out of the pack, swishing the stick like a wand. The wispy lichen floats beside him. Cedar dusts the tall boulders, the tree trunks, and me.

Frenchie

Pink Sun

The sun that had warmed Frenchie and dried his shirt, underpants, and hair was huge now. And pink. Suppertime sun. Frenchie looked around him. He did not want to eat lichens, little green pine needles, or tree bark. So he inched right to the edge of the flat spot that held him, made a cup with one hand, and slurped cold water from the quarry. He spilled. But there was lots more if he wanted it.

He scooted himself back, away from the edge, careful to set his hurting parts down gently. He tucked up and wrapped his arms over his head. He peeked out through the space between his elbows. The pink sun made a rosy glow on the dark water of the quarry.

And the rocks. Big.

And the stones. Small.

Down, down, down, the pink sun dropped. Frenchie watched it all the way.

Slice.

Sliver.

Dash.

Done.

Aurora

Twilight

The trees aren't so thick, and the boulders aren't as huge. Looks like another meadow up ahead.

"Close, close," Pop tells us. He looks at the map on the phone. "One last property to cross. We should see the road soon."

Soon is usually a good word. But when Pop says it now, I tug on the ends of my hair and don't let go. All seems lost. I feel lost. *Soon* means we'll stop. How can we do that when we haven't found Frenchie?

Then I see something. "Wait. What is that?" My heart pumps, like it's starting me up. "There's something in the trees!" I bound forward.

I keep it in my sights. It's round enough to be a person's head!

Right size!

Right height!

And is it moving? I swear I see it moving.

I keep clawing forward.

Frenchie? Frenchie? Please be you!

But it isn't Frenchie. It's a ball-shaped burl on a tree trunk. I drag my fingers across it—rough, old brain-shaped thing. How could I mistake a bump of bark for my best friend?

Mom and Pop and Gracia catch up to me.

Mom puts her hands on my shoulders, give them a squeeze. "Did you meet with a trickster, my girl?"

"Yeah," I mumble. "Sorry. Sorry, Gracia."

"Don't be," she says. "It's hope that makes us see things. And I won't lose hope."

We reach the roadside, and we can see other searchers heading to the school. Not far. Gracia pauses. She looks at the horizon line. The sun is gone. A narrow streak of pink is left behind.

"Gracia?" Mom asks. "What is it?"

"The twilight," she says, looking up and all around. "Seems so *inky*."

And I bet she is thinking what I am thinking: her no-talk boy, her son, is somewhere out there in the almost dark.

Aurora

Dinner Stop

When we get to the Fire and Rec Center there is food. A lot of food. And long tables all set up. This could be a party. Except it's not. The volunteers tell us, "Take a plate. Please eat!" Groups of searchers start to fill the tables, stepping over the benches with their full plates in their hands. I don't think I've ever seen the center so busy.

Some of the food is not what we eat, like there must be a hundred boiled hot dogs and big squirty jugs of ketchup and relish. There are two giant jars of the Picklonious Deli's famous sour pickles. Any other time, I'd go elbow-deep for one of those. Tonight, I don't want anything.

Mom tries. She steers me toward a tray of mac and

cheese. She spoons some out for Cedar, even though she usually keeps him from eating too much dairy—like it will gum up his ears or something. "Aurora? Some for you too?"

I shake my head.

"Baked beans? How about a scoop? This is dinner. You should try to eat some—"

I flap my hand at her. "I'll get us a table," I say.

I find a nice clean one. Some older kids are clearing and wiping. I sit down on the long bench. I fold my arms on the tabletop and set my forehead on them. I stare down at my lap and my feet. My legs are tired. The weird way. Where they can't stop moving. I let them swing, and I breathe. The space around my face fills with my own warm air. It's noisy on every side of me. I hear, but don't listen. Don't have to. No one is talking to me.

My mind talks to itself—and to Frenchie.

What the heck? Where did you go?

And why?

Was it a bird? When?

Couldn't you have waited?

I ask myself, what have I not thought of? Or just forgotten? Frenchie gets ideas—kind of the same way I sometimes blurt—and suddenly, he slips away. Whenever we've had to look for him—like fetch him for supper— we find him nearby, under the overhang at the A-frame, or staring up a tree beside the house. Or sitting with eyes closed, loving the feel of the sun on his face down at Pebble Nest.

What could've been different about today?

I feel somebody slip onto the bench beside me—two somebodies, one on each side. I feel a hug, arms close around my ribs. I see the sleeve of a bright pink silk tunic top wrapping across my middle. Leena. She squeezes me. On my other side, Joanie puts an arm on my shoulders. Her fingers pat my neck.

"Hi," I say. I feel kind of bad for not picking up my head, and I know my neck must be the sweatiest, dirtiest thing on the planet.

Then I see something even dirtier under the table across from me: a pair of caked-up work boots and muddy cuffs.

A deep voice asks, "Is she okay?" I keep my face in my warm space but think the voice is asking about me—am I okay.

"She misses her friend," says Leena.

"Frenchie Livernois is her bestie. And she's his," Joanie adds.

Now I wonder who wants to know.

I feel a hand on my forearm. Rough fingers. I pick up my head. Carney Huggins. Lucky for him, I have no words, and for sure, no loud ones.

"Hey, Aurora," he says, "want pie?" He slides a paper

bowl full of crackled-up blueberry pie right against my arm and sticks a spoon into it for me. I could cry. But I'm not a crier.

"Thanks," I say. I'm raspy as a frog. "I heard you're the one who saw him."

"Wild coincidence," he says, and he shakes his head.

"And he was fine? Or at least he looked okay?" I ask.

"I only got a quick look. But I think so." Carney nods. "So, listen, keep your chin up, okay?" He doesn't stick around but turns back to wave as he goes.

Mom and Pop and Gracia and Cedar come join Leena and Joanie and me. I don't feel good, exactly, but I do feel surrounded by good people.

Everyone is eating, and I try a bite of the mac and cheese that Mom pushes at me. I pick at it, and I see Gracia picking too. She makes a little *yum-yuck* face at me, as if to say it's good but who can eat? She feels the way I feel.

Leena's big sister, Zenia, comes over with a plate of potato-and-pea samosas. "Hey, guys. An offering from the food truck," she says. She stays because Cedar is making everyone laugh. He pinches at a slippery baked bean with his fingers and chases it around his plate.

Leena says, "Aurora, I'm wrapping a samosa for you, to go."

Joanie runs off and comes back with two spoons. She hands one to Leena. "Come on, Aurora, grab your spoon. We're going to help you eat that pie."

Later, Anzie Maylord comes over to say goodbye. "Gracia, if you hear anything in the night, no matter what time, please call," she says. "We are close by. Otherwise, we will see you all in the morning. First light."

Pop asks if Anzie could give him a ride to our minivan, which is still parked at the side of Punkinville Road.

"Sure! We've got the truck, but we'll squeeze you in," says Anzie. "I'll take the middle."

I watch Pop go. The back of his shirt is pressed with the shape of Cedar's carrier straps. Carney holds the door open for Pop and Anzie, then he looks over his shoulder at me and gives me a nod.

Mom says we should clean up our table and be ready for when Pop gets back. I'm glad to have something to do. I gather up our mess and make my way to the dish tubs and trash cans. While I am there, I hear my name.

"Aurora!" It's Mr. Menkis, Frenchie's classroom aide. He motions to me. He's sitting at a table with a man and a woman. They are young, like Mr. Menkis, but taller. I go to them and right away, I see that they have a whole lot of gear with them. Serious outdoorsy stuff, like packs with neon reflectors, and loops of rope and straps hitched up to carabiners.

Mr. Menkis introduces us. "Aurora, meet my friends, Mr. Reesick and Ms. Schneizik."

"Really?" I say. "Sheesh. Your friends rhyme." All three of them let out snorts.

"I know!" Mr. Menkis says. "What were the chances? Hey, guys, Aurora is Frenchie's best friend. I am talking *superlative*." It sounds like something good, so I smile.

Mr. Reesick tells me, "Hey, Aurora, I know you have to call him Mr. Menkis because he's a teacher. But you can call me Dave."

Ms. Schneizik points to herself and hurries a swallow. "And I'm Jordanna," she says. "We know this has been a hard day. So sorry."

Dave says, "But listen, we are going out right after we fuel up here."

"Out? To look for Frenchie?"

"Yep."

"In the dark?" I ask.

"Yep." Jordanna taps her headlamp and it flashes. She pats her pack and a row of lights blinks across the strap.

"Dave and Jordanna are my climbing buddies," Mr. Menkis tells me. "We took search-and-rescue training together this summer."

"For real?" I can hardly believe my ears.

"Yep. I called them to come help us find Frenchie."

"All for one and one for all!" Jordanna pumps her fist.

"Can you train me?" I ask. "Can I go out there with you?"

"I wish," Mr. Menkis says. "But I'm afraid there is more to it than we could teach you in one night. A lot of parts, and equipment, and you have to be eighteen."

251

"Yeah. I figured," I say. "How long are you going to search?"

"Through the night," says Dave.

"Until when?"

"Until we find him," Mr. Menkis says. He holds up his elbow, and I knock it with mine.

Aurora

Before Bed

"How to get through these next hours until day break," Gracia says. Her voice is shaky. She holds her hands in two small fists against her chest. Her face is a map of worry lines.

"Stay here with us," Mom tells her.

"We'll make up the sofa for you," Pop tells her.

"Or my bed," I say. "You can have my bed tonight." I mean it.

"Thank you. But I need to be home in case Frenchie turns up—"

"And he could!" I sit straight when I say it. I want it to be true. "Sorry for interrupting, but he knows the way home. He always does."

Silently, I think, then why isn't he back? And then I hear it in my mind, the bad thing I have not been able to say.

What if it's because he can't get back?

Gracia comes to me, her arms open. She's forcing a tiny smile, I can tell.

"Quick hug, Aurora?" she asks, which is like promising not to overdo it, because she knows I'm a short hugger, same as she knows Frenchie rarely takes a hug at all.

"For good luck," she adds. We squeeze each other, and I make sure I don't let go first.

Then Mom walks Gracia next door. Their shoulders touch the entire way; I see them in the light from the porch lamp. Reminds me of the day we all met at the bus stop, the day all of us started to be best friends.

It's impossible, I think. Impossible for us to go to our beds knowing that Frenchie is not in his.

Frenchie

The Dream

Frenchie Livernois fell asleep in the dark right where he was, all hunkered up close to the wall of the narrow ledge. Soon he was dreaming. In the dream, he was very small. Small enough to be sitting way down inside of a bowl a lot like the one Ed Petrequin used when he made pancakes in the kitchen at Aurora's house. The needlepoint purse was high and away. Frenchie wanted his birds. So he called to them. He made sounds in his dream.

One by one papers came blowing out of the purse. One by one birds lifted off the papers into the air. They flew. One by one they came down into the bottom of the bowl and perched where Frenchie could see them *so well*. He saw their knees tucked up under their wings. He saw every feather stripe. And the holes where the feathers grew out of the bird skin. He heard the birds breathing through their hollow bones. He saw their purple beating hearts. And he saw their long naked bird toes right next to his.

Aurora

Bedtime

Mom puts Cedar down for the night. She checks with me to see if I want anything to eat. I don't. She sends me to the shower. I soap up my arms and legs and scrub about a hundred fresh bug bites and scratches clean. Then I let the water run on my face and my sweaty neck. I get it all done fast—too fast. Because the only thing left to do then is go to bed. Before they send me upstairs, Mom and Pop want us to make up a list of positives.

"Good luck," I say. Mom starts.

"This night is unseasonably warm, and clear," she says. "Frenchie might feel a little chilly, but he's safe from bad weather."

"He's a strong boy and a good hiker," says Pop.

"Mr. Menkis and his two friends will search through the night," I say. "So at least somebody is out there. It makes me feel like Frenchie is less alone."

"Agree," says Mom, and Pop nods. "And Frenchie likes being outdoors—and he even loves the night sky," Mom adds.

"Yeah. And like Gracia said, he's not as worried about himself as we are about him. I think it's true." I twist the hem of my sleep shirt and remember back on some of the places we searched today. There are pictures in my mind, like Frenchie tucked into a circle of ferns. Or grass. His own nest.

"Maybe if we think of that we can relax enough to get some sleep," Mom says. "Then we'll be better in the morning. Better for Frenchie."

I get into my own bed, gather my quilt close, and I think I will sleep. But my legs hiked all day, and they are still hiking now. They kick out all their own, like I brought somebody else's legs to bed with me. I press my elbows to my ribs, try to make myself still. My mind sees Frenchie in all the places we've been, and it makes me wonder if we'll be in those places together again. Ever. Why did this happen? Why can't we be having a campout together right now? Why can't he be with his mom next door where he belongs? How long can I lie here not sleeping?

My bedsheet looks like a fat twist of rope. My quilt is in a bunch. I sit up and wonder where the comfortable spot in my bed has gone—where's the place that usually holds on to me?

I go downstairs and find Pop snoozing in the recliner. Mom is on the couch, sipping a mug of tea.

"Aurora," she whispers. She pats the spot beside her with her hand. I settle next to her and pull my feet up. I inch my toes close to Mom's thigh, and she lets me tuck them under where it's warm, and where she can weigh them down for me so they'll stop twitching. She sets down her tea and wraps me with one arm. We don't speak, not at first. I sit by her warm side and think about everything, everything, everything. This day . . .

"I'm scared, Mom. And I really miss him."

"Aurora . . ." She pulls me close, and I let her. "I know. I'm so, so sorry."

"Mom, you know how Frenchie likes birds? And the sun? And even the night sky, like you said."

"Yes," Mom says, and I can hear her smiling.

"I think he likes tree leaves and clouds and even rain too. Everything that is up, off the earth." I turn to look up at her. "It's like that's where his big world is."

"Hmm . . . ," says Mom. "I've always thought how positive he looks when he tilts his face up." She raises her chin the way Frenchie does.

"I hate this, Mom. I lie in my bed just waiting for morning. . . ."

"These are the hardest hours of anyone's life." Mom's

lips are on my head. She's twirling a loose piece of my hair. I can almost never sit still for someone fussing with me that way. But tonight, I do.

"Mom, promise me we will go back to searching. Like Anzie said, first light."

"We will." It's Pop who answers.

"Did we wake you, Pop?"

"Naw, not really. I've been in and out," he says. "Been thinking . . ."

"About what?"

"Well, Frenchie, of course, and Gracia. Poor Gracia. But also, about tomorrow because it's going to be tricky. At some point we have to go deal with Pebble Nest."

"Right." Mom sighs.

"Pebble Nest?" I sit up. "What about it?" Then I remember. "Oh. Tomorrow is Saturday. Well, forget it!" I say. "We can't do the cleaning. Call the renters. Tell them the deal's off."

"Can't do that. The house has to be made ready," Pop says, but he is shaking his head like he wishes that wasn't so. "We can't neglect our business."

"But what about Frenchie!" I say it loudly. Mom puts her hand on my knee.

"Hang on, now," she says. "We will all go back to the search first thing in the morning. That is a given," Mom says, and Pop agrees with her. But then they talk about Pebble Nest, and how maybe Mom should leave the search around noon with Cedar and give Pop's back a rest from the carrier pack. Or should Pop go? Would starting at noon give anyone enough time to do all the cleaning and make all the beds on their own? Would Cedar be wild and cranky? Maybe Pop and I should keep Cedar and . . .

They keep discussing.

I rub my face with my hands. I think about tomorrow. All the impossible parts. Suddenly, I know that Mom *cannot* go to Pebble Nest.

I interrupt them.

"It has to be Pop," I say. "I'll go with him, and we'll take Cedar too." My parents are both looking at me and listening. "Gracia has to stay with the search because Frenchie is her boy. And Mom has to stay with Gracia." I look right at Mom. "She needs you the most."

"That's good reasoning," says Pop.

"So thoughtful," says Mom.

"Pop, promise me we'll work really fast when we get there." A big jaw-stretcher of a yawn catches me. I lean on Mom.

"Never faster," Pop says, and I know he means it.

Frenchie

Waking and Remembering

Frenchie opened his eyes as darkness was going away. His sleep was going away too.

He sat on the flat ledge. He remembered how he came down. And lost his shoes. And the needlepoint purse with all his birds. He didn't have pants now. He had cool white legs. He had one arm wrapped around them. His other hand held tight to a tiny pine tree that had its root stuck into the rock.

Frenchie wanted some sun on him. But the high, high rock at his back kept him wrapped in shade. If he could get home, the sun would be there, he was sure. He knew the way. But there was no path here where he was. No place to take a step. No way to go up. He held on to the pine and leaned forward—only a little because it hurt to unbend his body. He looked all around as far he could see.

He remembered one more thing that he had lost. That piebald deer.

Aurora

First Light

We are up at first light, and back at the Fire and Rec Center before 6:00 a.m. People are pouring in, a swarm of orange vests. Way more people than yesterday. I remember that it is Saturday. More people are available. The check-in is organized.

Chief Nash speaks through the bullhorn. "Please see a volunteer for instructions at the tables marked with an *A*. Move on to tables marked *B* if you'd like one of our student volunteers from the high school to help you download the tracking app. . . . Please refer to the large screen to understand the scope of our search thus far."

I cover my ears and move away. That bullhorn is not morning-friendly. Pop is handing coffees to Mom and

Gracia. Cedar is sprinting through the crowd from one wall of the Fire and Rec Center to the other. I could stop him. But people smile every time he weaves by. Besides, Mom and Pop are keeping an eye on him.

There is food. Again. Breakfast.

I do a double take when I spot Darleen Dombroski. It looks like she is in charge of a bagel basket. I'm so tired my gaze turns into a stare.

I'm thinking about Frenchie. Best days. Like, when Cedar came home. And family dinners and pancake Sundays. Bird hounding and rock hounding, and me cheering Frenchie on the day he learned to float. Him going along with me, the times we trailed the piebald deer. And him knowing the way home. Having a true friend—the thing I am aching for this morning.

I blink. There's Darleen. And her bagel basket. She sees me seeing her. I bite my bottom lip. Darleen doesn't have a person like Frenchie Livernois.

Poor Darleen. I mean it, for real. *Poor Darleen.*

She doesn't know how good that can be. She can't even ache like I'm aching right now. But she still came here today.

I go on over to her.

"Hey," I say. "I'm sorry you got all scratched up yesterday. That puckabrush will get you if you don't watch out. And sometimes it just gets you anyway, huh?"

She dips her head a little and nods.

"I got a bee sting too!" she squeaks, as if that sting is still happening right now.

"Oh yeah? Super sorry," I say. "It's hard out there," I tell her. "It means a bunch that you came to help. Thanks."

"I'm helping indoors today," she says. She even smiles a little. "I'm going to serve lunch. It's a better assignment for me."

"Right. People will be huge-hungry!" I offer her a high five. She looks a little worried, but she takes it. Her eyelids flutter when our palms smack. I probably did that too hard. I decide to scoot back to my family.

"What do you think, Aurora?" Pop nods toward the table full of fruit, breakfast bars, and Darleen's bagels. "Want to grab some grub along with our assignment? You could stand to eat something, my girl."

I shrug. Then I'm saved by the bullhorn.

Chief Nash says something about a progress board up in the front of the room. I tell Pop, "I'm going to go see."

The word *progress* has me curious, but when I get to the Progress Board, I see that it's mostly the same stuff as yesterday. The list: missing boy, eleven years old, plaid shirt and tan pants, nonverbal, dark hair. They have added the LAST KNOWN POSITION at Punkinville Road, and another note that says they are dropping digital pins in areas that have been searched BUT (in big letters) they believe the SUBJECT (why not say Frenchie?) has been on the move.

I have to agree with the last part. Frenchie can walk for hours once you get him going—or once *something* gets him going. But when he decides he wants to go home, he does. So if he's on the move, why hasn't he *moved* home yet? It bothers me about like a bur caught in the arch of my shoe.

Here's another bother: if you ask me, "progress" would be having a lot more than the same list from yesterday with a few guesses added on. I stand in front of that board, shifting my weight from foot to foot.

"Pfft!" I say. "How do we even know it's *progress* until we actually find him?" I say this to no one, except there is a woman standing beside me, and I'm pretty sure she hears me. I watch her tie a bandanna around her close black hair. Then she adjusts her glasses on her nose and looks back at me. We both open our mouths and say, "Oh!"

Loud as a girl with a bullhorn, I say, "Hey! You're the Nuthatch Lady!"

"Yes, I guess I am," she says.

"Yeah! You're, umm . . . Sheree! Right? You gave Frenchie Livernois the Audubon print. You broke up that set of six for him and left yourself with five. And now you're here to help find him?" I ask. "Did you know that's who we're looking for?"

"Yes. I saw his picture on the news last night. I recognized him right away. The boy who loves birds. I've never forgotten him. I guess I feel connected."

"You are," I say. "I see you're not wearing your flat little-shop shoes today."

"Oh no. Hikers all the way," she says.

"Good thing," I say. I am about to tell her more when Mr. Menkis stops on his way out.

"Ready, Aurora?" he asks. "It's a brand-new day." He bounces in place to settle his pack on his shoulders. His carabiners jingle, and his ropes swing.

"I'm ready," I say. "Mr. Menkis, did you really search all night?"

"We did. Sorry I can't tell you that we found him," he says.

"I know you tried. Did you sleep?"

"Hmm . . . no. But my energy is up," he says. "I'm optimistic. We have a lot more help today. Did you hear? There's a group of mountain bikers, and the cross-country team from the high school is here. Some folks from an ATV club got special permission to ride some of the trails north of the school. Dave and Jordanna are still with me, right outside. And you're here," he says. He smiles at the Nuthatch Lady and me, then waves as he pushes on the door.

"And you're here too." I cup my hands and send him an echo. Then I think, Yep, we're both here. Mr. Menkis and Aurora Petrequin. The ones who lost Frenchie Livernois. And now we're going to be a part of finding of him. With lots of help.

I turn to the Nuthatch Lady. Sheree.

"Thanks for coming. I mean, a lot, a lot, a lot. And thanks for that nuthatch print. Frenchie loves it. Did you get a bagel? Do you like coffee? Right over there. It's free." I point her in the right direction, and when I do, I feel a little burst in my chest. It's like a firework lighting up.

I feel optimistic. Like Mr. Menkis said.

Maxine Grindel

Orientation at the Fire and Rec

Maxine Grindel felt bolstered when she saw the crowd at the Fire and Rec Center so early in the morning. She was relieved to finally join the search party. Her head was free of the previous day's cobwebs—not drowsy in the least. She was keenly worried about that boy, and could not stop picturing him, so slight and silent. So vulnerable. And already he'd spent an entire night outside on his own.

He'll be found today, she told herself with resolve. Safe and sound.

In the next second a speeding toddler with a headful of dark curls brushed by Maxine. She instinctively clutched her bandaged finger to her chest. (It would hurt like the dickens if it got bumped.) She heard the little one laughing, a mingle of mischief and glee. An older child was right behind him, giving chase, and insisting that it was time for them to go.

"Mom and Pop want you!" the older girl called.

If Maxine had gotten a better look, she might have recognized the chaser as the talkative girl who came by Mrs. Thrift's booth at Baker's Field two Julys ago. Maxine might have remembered that she was the girl who had been with the now-missing boy the day his soft-spoken momma had bought him the needlepoint purse.

Instead, Maxine and Dudley continued on their way to Table A for the brief orientation. Maxine recognized Jewell Laramie right away. She knew they'd lucked into a competent instruction-giver. Jewell had a reputation: she was a hunter; she knew the woods. This morning, she was on the job as Maxine and Dudley approached.

Jewell spoke between gulps of coffee. She explained about the tracking system, and about the significance of the last known position.

"I shared a hunch yesterday," Jewell confided as she referred Maxine and Dudley to the map on the screen. "The boy was seen crossing there at Punkinville Road, and I happen to know there is an identifiable deer path right there. Just waiting for a kiddo to come along, if you know what I'm saying." (Maxine wasn't entirely sure, but she nodded nonetheless.) "You can see where the search has been focused, going on up through town roughly east to west, on a bit of a diagonal." Jewell resketched the highlighted line with her finger. "We've been thorough. The catch is, the timing. It's late summer, and in the world of white-tailed deer, that means the does have been out on their own, fattening up for mating season. They've cut a lot of little trails to get to their favorite edibles and lie-downs."

"Umm-hmm. So we have a lot of those little trails to search," Dudley said with a nod.

Maxine squinted at the large screen. "Look at that, Dudley. That main trail goes right beside our yard! See the shape of the lot? That's us. I never knew . . ."

"Ah. You're on a main thoroughfare," Jewell said.

"And we do see deer," Maxine said. "Six to eight at a time." She paused a moment. "Speaking of deer," she began to address Jewell, who would surely be interested, even though she seemed to be looking past Maxine now, "I saw one at our bird feeder yesterday, and it had the most amazing spotted co—"

"Yut, yut. So sorry to cut you off, Maxine," Jewell interrupted. "I'm seeing quite a bottleneck at the door, folks coming my way. I'm afraid I've got to move you on over to Table B. The kiddos will help you put the search app onto your phone." She pointed, took a sip of coffee, and waved to the students, seemingly all in one motion.

"Little help here for these folks. Yut, yut. Again, apologies, Maxine."

"Not at all, Jewell! We are on a mission here," Maxine said. She cupped her injured finger close again, and she and Dudley shuffled along to Table B.

Aurora

Forward, Then Back

I'm eating the bagel that Pop brought for me. I chew in time with my footsteps and wash each bite down with a gulp from my water bottle.

You felt optimistic! Now stay optimistic! I tell myself this again and again.

Trouble is, the day feels cut short every way I look at it. Pop and I cannot go far today. We will need to head back to the car and go to Pebble Nest. What if we don't find Frenchie before then? Then after we finish cleaning, we'll be starting all over again—and who knows where that'll be?

"Wherever they drop us a pin," I mumble to myself. "But then how long before the sun is gone again?"

Frenchie cannot stay out another night. We have to do better.

I think about all the times I have messed up and had to fix something. What did I do? My only answer: I tried harder. So here I am wondering, how can I search harder? Do I stomp my feet down firmer? Open my eyes wider? (I know it's ridiculous, but I try it anyway.) How do I do more than I'm doing?

"Hey, can I go off the trail?" I ask. "I'll stay with you. I'll just be about ten feet away."

"What's your purpose?" Mom asks.

"To walk wider," I tell her. I spread my arms open. "To see more."

"Sure. Give it a try," Moms says. "But do keep up, Aurora."

I lunge into the puckabrush, even if the hiking isn't as easy—and it's not. Even if it means more scrapes and scratches—and it does. I call for Frenchie. I try to tweet the way he does—almost like an oriole. I see birds, and I watch where they go until I can't see them anymore. I flap my arms, wishing I could be an eye in the sky.

There are other searchers nearby, covering side trails, nooks, and crannies. I see their heads and shoulders. I cover my mouth with my hand and hold back a bagel burp. Nobody needs to hear what's been building in my stomach.

The sun is moving up in the sky. I want Pop to forget

about Pebble Nest. But I know he's watching the time. I am dreading that hike back to the car.

I have a good thought: there are so many people who want to bring Frenchie home. He gets ignored a lot, it's true. He's the kid nobody is sure what do with. But this morning, whole families from school arrived at the center as we were leaving. And people like Sheree, the Nuthatch Lady. She remembered him! How *wow* is that? I didn't actually see Mrs. Thrift with my own eyes, but I saw her camper van in the lot. And Anzie's truck was there. Leena and the whole Virani family said they'd join the search today, and Joanie and her mom too. Even Darleen had found her own best way to help.

The time comes. No trace of Frenchie, but Pop and Cedar and I have to turn back. We check the charge on Gracia's phone and make sure the app is working. We hug each other, then we split up.

I follow behind Pop, looking right and left and up, while Cedar bobbles in the pack. I can tell Pop is worried that he hasn't left enough time to spruce up Pebble Nest before 3:00 p.m., when the new guests will arrive.

"Pop, we'll get it all done!" I call up to him. "I'm already stripping beds. In my mind."

"What's that? The 'think' system?" He laughs. He is taking long strides. I try to match him but I have to double step.

"Ya know, retracing doesn't mean we stop searching,"

I say. "Jewell was retracing on purpose yesterday. Remember?"

"Right, my girl," he says.

That's all I need to hear. I believe it: there is a chance we will find Frenchie. Wouldn't that be something? I can picture it: suddenly he comes out onto the path with his plaid shirt all tucked in.

The geode swings inside the pocket of my shorts. I keep it going, and I keep up with Pop. I call my friend's name. I look left and right—

Boof! I walk my face smack into the back of Pop, and the carrier. I plant my eye into the heel of Cedar's sneaker.

"Ow!" I spin and grab my face.

Pop stumbles forward, on account of me bashing into him, then turns around. "Oh, girl! Are you all right?" I squirm while he does a close-up check.

"It's fine," I say, though my eye is aching and does *not* want to be pried open.

"'Kay, Awoh-woh?"

"Yeah, Cedar Tree," I grumble. I reach up and give him a pat. "I'm okay."

But I am not.

I am miserable, and it isn't about the bump in the eye. It's about this feeling I have that the three of us are heading in the wrong direction now. Like Frenchie's somewhere behind us. The only thing good about that is Mom and Gracia are behind us now too.

Aurora

Putting a Fast Shine on Pebble Nest

We rush in the door with our baskets of fresh sheets and towels and the empty recycling bins. Pop and I hold our breath and do a quick scan. I let out a cheer, because the Poets of Guilford have left Pebble Nest in tip-top shape.

"Phew! And glory!" says Pop.

I run to up the stairs to check the bedrooms. I call down. "The poets stripped their own beds!"

"Oh, love those poets! Love them!" He sings it out loudly. He has to. Cedar is banging on the piano down in the living room. "Start with the sinks and tubs, will you?" Pop hollers. "I'll be up in a minute, and we'll make the beds together."

I scrub a shine onto every inch of porcelain. I dust the night stands and dressers and empty all the wastepaper cans into one. When Cedar comes up the stairs with the duster, I send him around all the edges. "Do a good job. Like Frenchie," I say.

He looks at me funny. Like he's concentrating. He says, "En-chee."

"Yep, Frrr-enchie," I say. Mom wants us to try to get Cedar to hear the difference.

"En-chee en bye-baw."

"Bye-baw? That again?" I snort a laugh. Cedar looks back at me, his eyes narrow. He whispers it one more time.

"Bye-baw."

I shake my head. "Come on, Cedar Tree. We have work to do."

"En beech-en-yoks?" he asks. This one I know: And beach and rocks?

"Yep, yep. We'll go down to the water as soon as we finish here. But only for a few minutes. Understand?"

He nods, a big nod.

"'Kay, Awoh-woh."

Ezelda Trink

Something Autumnal

On Saturday afternoon, Ezelda Trink rested her mug of tea on the split rail fence and looked out over the deep quarry pond. Tea at three, as it should be. What a relief to have things back to normal after yesterday's no-good shelf collapse in the studio. All those leather-hard pots in pieces on the floor. She'd planned to fire them today, dang it all. Instead, she'd pushed the ruins all back into the vat to soak. A few days, and they'd all be soft clay again.

"Could've been worse," she muttered. She cupped her mug in her hands, admired the sea-green glaze for a moment. She looked out across the still dark water of the pit quarry, and to the broad, high wall of granite beyond.

Something caught her eye. Way up, there was a square of color. It was reddish, not bright but autumnal perhaps, set off by the backdrop of gray granite.

Ezelda reached into the wooden box on the post and lifted out the binoculars.

"These old eyes . . ." She mumbled as she hunted through the lenses for that claret-colored square. There! There it was! A leafy-patterned piece of fabric. Some sort of handbag, was it? Embroidery? Needlepoint? Ezelda could see that it was dangling by its strap on a skinny, bent sapling. There was something familiar about it.

Ezelda scoffed. People were always roaring through that parcel of town land on motorbikes or snowmobiles and stopping up there to catch the view over her quarry. Often, they'd stay and watch the sunset. She didn't mind that. Beauty belonged to everyone. But she *did* mind the campfires, often left burning up on the rocks; she *did* mind when people tossed trash and other unwanteds over the edge. Her quarry was *not* a dump. Most of all, she feared someone would make a mistake and either drive or dive off that ledge. The pit quarry was legendarily deep and perilous, with its projections of granite, and who-knew-what-else rusting away down below.

Whoever had tossed that bag had failed to give it a good enough fling. "Got it hung up on that twiggy tree, now did ya?" Ezelda mused. She kept her eyes pressed against the cool circles of her binoculars, and traced the path the handbag would have taken had it fallen all the way down. There was the bit of ledge there at the water's edge—

"My stars!" Ezelda Trink said right out loud. "What is that?"

Aurora

Last Sweep

"Remember, Cedar, we can't stay long. So soak it in now." He grabs two fists full of pebbles and throws them into the water. He kneels and scrapes more into a pile. I kneel beside him. I close my eyes. Let the breeze blow two days' worth of uncombed hair out of my face.

Pebble Nest, you are the best.

But for the first time in my life I feel restless on this beach. I need to go. Pop is inside doing the last sweep before we go rejoin the search.

Cedar's mound of pebbles shines in the sun. Most Saturdays, I am here with Frenchie hunting for tourmaline in the surf. I never find any. I like the hunting. I like that Frenchie is beside me. I pull my half of the geode out of my pocket, nestle it into the tiny pebbles. I cup water in my hands and let it spill into the miniature crater.

I turn my face up to the sun. September bright. And then everything hurts. My middle cramps up, like my own heart has tied itself into a knot. And now it's pulling extra hard.

I want him back!

Ezelda Trink

Through the Lens

Ezelda peered at the small-looking someone, all tucked up on the low, narrow ledge of granite far across the water. It was his legs, pale as fish bellies, that had caught her eye, even before the bands of bright red that ran through his plaid shirt. Hadn't that boy visited the quarry before? With a girl about the same age? Hard to tell from this distance—and through a cloudy old set of binocular lenses.

Slowly, it all came back to her. About a year ago, a writer had brought her family and friends. She wrote a quarry story. The girl had been a ripe talker. The boy couldn't or wouldn't. He'd had that needlepoint pocketbook with him—stuffed full of bird pictures.

Yes! He was all about birds. That's what the girl had said.

Through the binoculars Ezelda could see the boy clinging to a white pine sapling that had taken root on the granite shelf. How had he gotten there? She raised her hand to signal him. "Are you hurt?" she called. Her voice bounced back to her. Then she remembered, he wouldn't answer.

Ezelda bit her knuckle. It was going to be near impossible to reach that boy. No one should climb that bank of grout—too jagged, too shifty—let alone portage a rescue float over it. And then back again? Ezelda thought not.

"Oh! Say! Young one! Could you wave to let me know that you're all right?" she called.

The boy sat still.

"I'm getting help! Don't move!"

Ezelda pulled her phone from her canvas apron. She hurried to the clearing by the studio. As soon as she saw that she had a signal—blessed signal—she poked in the numbers: 911.

Aurora

What Cedar Said

"I want him back!" I whisper. My jaw aches. "I want
Frenchie back." I bring my hands, still dripping with
water, up to my face. I feel it spilling down my front. I lean
down to scoop more. I stare into my hands, like I've got a
whole ocean cupped right here. I think of Frenchie. I see
him hiking, swimming, flapping his hands, and tweeting
like a bird. I make a list in my mind of all the tiny things
he understands—things most people wouldn't guess he
knew, like when the picture of the nuthatch is upside
down, how to fill a berry bucket faster than anyone, and
how to find his way home. . . .

Cedar pats me on my hip bone with his little hand. I
look down and see him standing on his toes, like he wants

to be right in my face. "En-chee," he says.

"Yeah, En-chee." I ruffle his hair. I don't care about correcting his speech. Not right now. I hold his hand and look into his serious brown eyes.

"En-chee en bye-baw," he says.

I shrug and I shake my head. I don't know what he's saying.

Frenchie and . . . something? Frenchie has my ball?

"En-chee en bye-baw!" Cedar says. He pushes those word at me so hard. Then he says, "Bye-baw *dee-yah*." Suddenly, I hear it.

"*Piebald deer!*" I say it out loud.

Cedar's eyes open wide.

"Are you saying piebald deer?"

His face breaks into an enormous grin.

"Aurora!" I hear Pop holler.

I squint toward the house. He barrels out the door, waving his phone in the air.

"It's Frenchie!" he calls.

I push my tongue between my lips. Taste the salt. What does Pop mean?

"They've spotted him!" Pop calls. He circles his arm. "They've found him!"

Found?

I gather Cedar in my arms and sweep down to grab my geode out of the pebbles. My little brother holds tight, and I run for the car while he giggles. Pop comes from the house. I hear the keys in his hand. We yank the car doors open.

I hitch Cedar into his car seat. My fingers are wet and shaking. I double-check his buckles, then click my own. "We're in, Pop! Both in!"

He spins the steering wheel with the heel of his hand and reverses.

I push my back against the seat and breath out. "Go! Go!" I say.

"Goh-goh!" cries Cedar.

Pop hits the gas. The gravel sprays back against the storage shed. We are off.

Aurora

Following Jewell Laramie

"Do you know where to go, Pop?"

"Roughly. He's out west of the school. At the back edge of quarry."

"The quarry! Where we went that time? But isn't that kind of far?"

"Not as the crow flies!" Pop says. "And we are to go in a different way, which is the part I'm not sure of. But north of the school, there's a town-owned parcel," he says. "Mom said something about snowmobile trails."

I'm craning to see out the front of the car. We reach the bottom of Bert Gray Road; I see a white Jeep tucked close to the pond, emergency lights flashing.

"Pop! That's Jewell! She's waving. I think she wants you to stop."

"Good gosh!" says Pop. He takes the turn and pulls off the road in front of the Jeep. He leans out the window and twists back to speak to Jewell. I can't catch a word she says. But I can hear Pop.

"Great! I'll be right behind you!" he says. He pulls his head back inside and waits while Jewell steers onto the road ahead of us.

"That Jewell is a gem!" Pop says. "She came down to lead us in. Phew!"

I take the phone and check the search app. There are no more highlights on the satellite view. No pie cuts, no assignments. There's just one pin now. It is off to the west behind Mountain View School.

This! This is the way I wanted to go!

Beside the pin is something that looks like a dark pool of water—the quarry! When I zoom in, I can see a dirt road that narrows into a windy, come-and-go line. It's the back way in. It's the path to Frenchie! And this feels like the longest trip up Bert Gray Road ever.

We take a turn just past the school, staying right behind Jewell's Jeep. We roll along a bumpy, gravelly road until it becomes too narrow for cars. Other vehicles have arrived before us, including emergency trucks from three different towns. The sight of them gives my heart a jump.

Jewell pulls over into the ferns behind them. Pop does the same. The second we park, I'm out of the car. I can see where to go—the trail is clear.

My feet hit the ground, and I run.

"Aurora! Wait! You wait!" Pop hollers. "Wait. For. Me."

I turn and see him tugging Cedar out of the car with one arm and jostling the carrier in his other.

"I can't!" I scream. I start fast-walking instead, arms swinging so hard they ache in the sockets. I hear the car door slam. I hear Pop yelling and Cedar calling to me. Then I hear Jewell Laramie.

She says, "Give me the baby, Ed. You need to run."

Aurora

Knots

Pop has me by the back of my shirt—like making a suitcase handle out of the armholes of my tank top. I haul him for at least a quarter mile. Three times he has told me, "There's a dangerous drop at the end of this trail. So help me, Aurora, you are *not* going off it."

"I won't! Pop, are you serious?" I say. "Think I don't want to be *alive* when I see Frenchie again?"

We see people up ahead, and I pull Pop harder. I see the light of the sky behind them. It's not the same as a clearing. It's like Pop has been saying, we are coming to the place where the land drops away and the forest ends. I catch sight of Mom. She's been watching for us and now, *now*, Pop finally lets me go.

I run at Mom, and she runs at me. She catches me in a full-stop bear hug. She holds me tight. She walks me back a few steps. "He's all right; he's all right!" she says, her breath in my ear. I want to believe her, but she keeps me walking me backward. I'm scared—scared there is something she doesn't want me to see.

"Mom! Let me go!"

"No," she says. She is calm and firm. "Not until I know that you are safe, Aurora. Let me talk to you."

Pop catches up to us. "For the love of Pete, Aurora!" He leans over his knees and takes big breaths. "Listen to your mom." I look her in the eye.

"The edge is steep," Mom says. "Loose rocks and ledges. So, no more running, no rushing forward. Understand?"

"Promise." I nod. I let her see me take a deep breath. I relax my shoulders. She eases her grip on me.

"Frenchie is down below beside the water. He seems okay. It's so lucky." She smiles her really big Mom smile. "Mr. Menkis is with him. He's been looking him over and talking to an emergency medic here at the top. His friends and the fire chief are deciding about the best way to bring Frenchie out."

"Can I see him?"

"Yes. Come slowly. Gracia has a clear view from a little overlook. This way. She wants to see you."

Mom leads us along the ledge. We step down a little

way and to one side. Gracia gathers me in her arms. "How do you feel about heights?" she asks. She smiles a real smile, and her eyebrows arch up, almost like she's playing. "Here, here. Hug the tree trunk. One leg on each side for safety." She keeps her hands on my shoulders. Mom and Pop are close by. "That's it. Hang on tight. Look down," she says.

The first thing I notice is a flash of red. "His needlepoint purse! His birds!" I say, and Gracia nods. It's dangling by its strap on a bony old branch in the face of the rock.

"Look way below, beside the water," Gracia tells me.

Then I see Frenchie huddled there—but not shutting down. Mr. Menkis is close beside him. I let out a little gasp. I look at Gracia. "How?" I whisper. "I can't believe it."

"Nor can I," she says. We crouch down together, because lower feels safer, even if you are clamped tight to a very good tree. The lower I can be on this high piece of ground, the closer I am to Frenchie.

Mr. Menkis helps Frenchie to his feet—very slowly. I wonder how Frenchie feels about squeezing onto that patch of granite with Mr. Menkis. He never chooses to be so close.

"Frenchie's showing a lot of trust," Gracia says.

"Yes, and it's good to see that he can stand without support," says Mom.

They're right. But for me it's surprising to see my friend with his shirt tails hanging down his thighs. No tucked-in mushroom look. I wonder a lot of things: Did he take a swim and leave his pants somewhere? And is he hurting? His body looks hunched and stiff.

I'm dying to call down to him, but I press my lips together.

I take a second to look around. I know exactly where we are. We're high above Ezelda Trink's deepwater quarry. In the distance there's the bank of broken stone. Grout, she called it. I see the shallow swimming ponds and the picnic spot. I see Ezelda's clay studio, the old backhoe she calls Gorgeous, and her megaliths, which look not so mega from here. This is a big bowl in the earth, and we are up on the rim. There are a lot of us.

I see Anzie Maylord, and Mrs. Whilmer, our principal. Mr. Gessup is here. There are teachers and parents from town. There's a whole bunch of fire and rescue team members, and Mr. Menkis's friends, Dave and Jordanna.

Back beneath the trees, I see Cedar sitting on Jewell's hip—and Mrs. Thrift and her husband are playing with him. Mrs. Thrift has a wicked bandaged-up finger. She wiggles it to make Cedar laugh.

I lean toward Gracia, still sitting tight. "So many people," I say.

"So many helpers who want to see him safe." She shows me a wide smile.

Pop goes back and forth between our overlook and the spot where the fire and rescue team is gathered. "They're discussing two options," he says. "Either take him across the quarry or raise him up and out."

Just get him, already!

I let out a growl. Things are moving too slowly. I squeeze Gracia's hand. "How can you stand this?" I ask.

"I'm okay." Her voice is bright. "I can see my son, and he seems surprisingly well." We look down at him. I'm not sure if Frenchie has seen us. He's not that big on greetings, and besides, he's been keeping his head low. He touches the ropes Mr. Menkis is hitched to and gives the fat knots a close look the same way he studies his bird prints.

Mr. Menkis's friends come down around behind us. Chief Nash is with them, and some of the fire and rescue team members too. Dave sees me and gives me a quick wave and a fist pump. Turns out they want to borrow our view. We lean out of their way. But I'm not giving up this tree unless they make me.

They talk on speakerphone with Mr. Menkis, who looks up from below. They ask him what he sees. Is there a way to walk out? Does he think Frenchie could cross the quarry strapped to a backboard?

Uhh ... No ...

It's all I can do to keep quiet. Gracia rises to half standing. "He's hypersensitive to anything restraining or confining," she says. "That would not be the best ..."

"Heard that." Mr. Menkis's voice comes through. "I agree, with Mrs. Livernois. Besides, crossing appears not optimal. We'd need equipment. An inflatable. There's an unstable-looking hill of jagged stone. And a fair amount of terrain to cross on foot. Going up is a fraction of the distance. Frenchie is already interested in my ropes and harnesses. . . ."

That makes me think about Frenchie—the way he is.

"It has to be *up* . . . ," I whisper.

Then, because I am Aurora Pauline Petrequin, I blurt, "Pull him *up!*" My voice echoes off rock and water. "He loves *up!*"

I think that blurt was a good one. But then everyone starts talking at once again. Suddenly, a sharp whistle slices the air—the kind of whistle that comes zinging through someone's teeth and makes everyone go silent.

But who was it?

He's almost invisible, at first, leaning back against a tall pine, but there's Carney Huggins. He peels himself forward, uncrosses his arms.

"Listen to the girl," he says. He nods in my direction. "She knows that boy as well as anyone."

I give him a side smile.

He says, "Speak your piece, Aurora."

"Uh . . . okay. Well, I say *up* because that's Frenchie Livernois, all the way. He loves birds. And trees and leaves and sunshine and rain. If it was nighttime right now, he'd be staring at the stars or the moon, or even the way the clouds blow across the moon." I take a breath. "Up is perfect for Frenchie."

"I agree!" Gracia says. She waves her arm to be counted.

"And me!" says Mom. "*Up* makes sense."

Pop taps a knuckle on my head. "Well done."

Chief Nash is silent as he paces about. He strokes his chin. I know he doesn't want to make a mistake. He only wants to bring Frenchie out safely.

Meanwhile, Carney shows me a thumbs-up, and I give him one in return.

Finally, the fire chief says, "Okay. Bottom line, we have fewer obstacles if we bring him up. It's a go." He nods at Dave and Jordanna.

Yes!

"Let's do it!" says Dave. He speaks into his phone. "Tandem lift, Menkis. That's why we sent you down there in the first place, hey?" He turns to the Chief Nash. "Menkis is the lightest of the three of us, strong as heck, and he knows the kid."

"Spot-on," says Jordanna.

She tells the fire chief, "We spent the summer pulling each other out of ravines and up rock faces. Promise you, we can do this."

They send a harness and a helmet down for Frenchie, then begin to assemble the ropes up top. They are quiet and serious as they work, tying double figure-eight knots and hitching them to carabiners. When one of them finishes a knot, the other one checks it. They strap a pulley to a broad tree trunk and thread a line through it. They talk through the plan with the fire and rescue team.

We hear Jordanna call out, "Ready at the top!"

But, it's not so easy to get a kid like Frenchie into a rescue harness and a helmet. Those aren't the sorts of things he wants on him. Mr. Menkis takes his time. He shows Frenchie how to step into the harness. Frenchie leans away, like he doesn't like the idea—the webbing could pinch or feel scratchy.

I cup my hands around my mouth and call down loud enough that I think Frenchie might hear me. "It's like putting on your orange vest. But tighter. I know you don't like that. But the harness will keep you safe. We want you up here."

Finally, Frenchie picks up one bare foot at a time and steps them inside the leg loops. Mr. Menkis pulls the harness up. Frenchie slips his arms through the top straps.

"He gets it," I say. "He gets so much."

Mr. Menkis brings the straps over Frenchie's shoulders and clips the buckle at his chest. He connects the ropes from up top, lots of slow, careful checking. He settles a helmet on Frenchie's head and buckles the chin strap. The last thing he does is pull Frenchie close to him—like he's holding him in his lap. He lets his feet come off the ground, and Frenchie's come off too. They're dangling, and Frenchie begins to squirm. He grips the rope in the front of him like he'd rather cling there than sit back in the harness. Gracia worries that something is hurting him. She bites the tip of her thumb.

Mr. Menkis talks to Frenchie, right beside his ear. He takes a small square of paper from his pocket. I know it's the Bird of the Day, the one he would've given to him yesterday if Frenchie had made it to class. Frenchie holds the bird. He lets himself settle back a little, but he still grips the rope hard with one hand.

Mr. Menkis calls, "Ready!"

The lines tense, and they begin to inch up.

"Go, go, go, *stop*," Mr. Menkis calls. He cradles Frenchie and steers around a jutting piece of ledge with a touch of his boot.

"Go, go, go . . . and slow, slow . . ."

Dave and Jordanna pull the ropes on his command, with help from the rescue team. Steady-eddy, no scary catches or drops. It's like a dance that they have practiced.

Except for one thing: Frenchie grunts—not like he's afraid. More like he's uncomfortable.

"Easy," Mr. Menkis tells him. "Look up and see. We don't have far to go. Nice and easy."

"It's okay!" I call. "You're coming *up*, Frenchie! BE THE BIRD!" I stand and start flapping my hands. Pop grabs my shirt and pulls me back from the edge. I keep flapping, and I try to tweet the way Frenchie does. One by one, around the top of the rim of this big bowl in the earth, others start to do the same. Mom and Pop and Gracia, Anzie and Carney, Jewell, and Mrs. Thrift, and folks we don't even know, are all flapping. They're tweeting the best tweets they can. It's a chorus! Frenchie must be loving it.

Closer and closer they come. When they pass us, we leave our overlook and scramble up and catch a very good view of Frenchie as he touches back on earth, safe and sound.

Frenchie

Up to the High Place

The harness pressed on all the most hurting spots Frenchie had.

But he heard Aurora's voice. Single. Clear.

BE THE BIRD!

So he flew up with Mr. Menkis, right past the needle-point purse, and into a circle of birdsongs, at the top.

Frenchie and Mr. Menkis did not stay at the edge of the high place.

Edge is not a good place to stand.

Frenchie saw all the ones he knew best, and when he saw Aurora, he remembered about the piebald deer. She would want to see it. He looked past all the people and into the dark and sunny woods around him.

The deer was still lost.

Mr. Menkis let Frenchie go. Unhitched. Frenchie stepped out of the harness. Both arms. Foot, foot.

He stood still while Gracia put soft arms around him. She spoke into his neck and said what she always said when her eyes turned wet and shone.

"Sun. My. Sun. Love. You. So. Much. My. Sun."

The bright sideways light made Frenchie's eyelids flutter.

SUN SUN SUN.

Aurora

Our Huddle

Gracia hugs Frenchie. Then she hugs us. She grasps every hand of every person she can reach. "Thank you. Thank you for everything." She must say it fifty times, and I know she means it more than a hundred.

There's an ATV waiting to take Frenchie and Gracia out of the woods. Frenchie's walk is stiff—not the normal Frenchie walk. But he goes right to the ATV without help. Gracia climbs in and pats the spot beside her. He creeps onto the mat, hands and knees. But he won't sit down. He curls onto his side next to Gracia's hip and closes his eyes.

"Ed and Rene . . . , I'll call you shortly," Gracia promises. "Aurora, we'll see you very soon. Okay?"

I nod back. I take a tough breath in. I wish we could

take Frenchie home. Right now. But I get it. He has to be checked by a doctor.

Word is, there's already an ambulance waiting out on Bert Gray Road to take him to the emergency clinic in Ellsworth.

The fire and rescue team tuck a blanket around Frenchie.

"All good," says Chief Nash. He hops in beside the driver. I stand with Mom and Pop and Cedar—family huddle. We watch them roll away.

Aurora

Pack Out

The searchers and helpers begin to pack out in groups along the trail.

"I'm about ready for some supper." Someone chuckles.

"Hot shower for me," says another.

"Sure will sleep better tonight knowing the boy is safe."

Sleep. That'll be nice. Hardly ever happens to me but today, right now, I am bone-tired. I know I'm not the only one.

Mom and Pop stay and thank everyone, and so does Jewell. I'm keeping Cedar busy now. We pick up pine cones and make slings of our orange vests to carry them.

"Bye-coes," he says.

"P-p-pine cones," I tell him. I think about him saying bye-baw dee-yah. Piebald deer. But I still don't know why he said it and with such a serious look on his little face.

Anzie is saying goodbye to Mom and Pop now. Carney hangs off to one side. I'm looking at him and thinking about everything that happened yesterday. Suddenly, I realize, I have a question for Carney. I walk up to him.

"Hey," I say. I keep my voice low, and I get him to turn toward me so it's just us talking. "Remember when you saw that flash of plaid down on Punkinville Road yesterday morning?"

"Yep."

"Did I hear someone say you stopped your truck to let a deer cross the road?"

"Yeah. Well, I slammed on my brake because the deer jumped into the road."

"Well, did you get a good look at that deer?" I ask.

Carney raises his eyebrows.

"Did it have a spotted coat? And did it look like no other deer you have seen in your whole life?"

"That's the one." Carney nods.

"Which came first, the deer, or the flash of plaid?"

"The deer."

"Thanks," I say. "That's all I wanted to know."

Anzie has a quick side-hug for me. "Aurora, *you* were so strong today, and so important to this positive outcome. We are so happy! I know blueberry season is over, but we still want to see you at the farm. Promise you'll bring Frenchie and Cedar and all your friends up in the next couple of weeks for pumpkin picking. Okay?"

"Yeah," says Carney. He smiles a sly smile. "All you can carry home in your arms—for free!"

"Uhh . . . but pumpkins are heavy," I say.

"That's right!" He laughs, and Anzie thumps his arm with her knuckle.

"Then just wait!" I call after them. "I'll bring a big burlap sack!"

"I'll count on that!" Carney calls back.

Mrs. Thrift and her husband come to say goodbye, and I find out that she does have a *real* name: Maxine Grindel.

"Rest assured," Maxine tells us, "the emergency clinic will take great care of your friend. I was there myself, yesterday morning." She holds up her wrapped finger. "Say hello to Miss Mummy."

"S-so sorry," I say, trying not to laugh. Getting hurt isn't funny. But she's making a joke about it. I fake a little throat clearing. "Hey, do you think *Mrs. Thrift* can find a new needlepoint purse for Frenchie? Something a lot like the last one? I've got some allowance—"

"Save your money, Aurora!" Mr. Menkis jogs up. Frenchie's purse is swinging from his hand.

"You got it back! Woo-hoo!" I jump up, pop my vest, and send all my pine cones flying.

"Oh! It's been retrieved!" Maxine Grindel tries to clap, then remembers about her finger. Jewell is standing by, and she claps extra hard.

"Yep, went back down and unsnagged it. Piece of cake," Mr. Menkis says. He loops the purse toward me, and I catch it on the upswing. I hug it to my chest, but not too hard. I don't want to smash up Frenchie's birds. They've been through a lot.

"That's going to mean so much to Frenchie," Mom says. "And Gracia too."

"Aurora, you're in charge of making sure he gets it back, okay?" says Mr. Menkis.

"Promise," I say. I hang the purse across my body, over the top of my orange vest, like Frenchie would wear it.

We stay, and Jewell stays, until all the climbing ropes have been recoiled and packed up. We all thank Mr. Menkis, Dave, and Jordanna.

"I'll see you *right at your classroom door* on Monday morning," I say.

"You bet!" Mr. Menkis replies.

"Ready?" Jordanna hoists her pack. "We still have half a weekend, and guess what? We're going climbing!"

"After we sleep," says Dave.

"Oh, come on. Who needs sleep?" Jordanna wants to know. "Hup, two, three, four!"

We are laughing as they head off.

Now it's just Jewell and us. We sit on stumps and rocks

310

and look over the quarry, where the sun has turned into a glowing ball of hot pink again.

"Ahh . . . September sunsets," says Jewell. "Aren't they grand?"

For the next minute or so, we drink in the peace. Even Cedar settles against Mom's legs, with his belly out and his vest lumpy with pine cones. We watch the sun touch the horizon.

Soon, Jewell stands and stretches and sighs a noisy sigh. "Time for me to take my leave. Best be out of the wilds before sundown," she adds.

"We're right behind you. So long, Jewell." Mom and Pop thank her for meeting us on the road, and for taking care of Cedar. She has been a good friend.

We stay a few more minutes. I feel like my feet are planted in this place. Maybe it's because we're standing here where things went wicked wrong, and then got so much better, and now we want to keep everything like it is for as long as we can. Or maybe it's taking these few more minutes for us to believe that it's really over.

We lift our tired selves onto our feet and start down the trail, with the rosy glow of the low sun at our backs.

Aurora

The Spotted Woods

Mom and Pop and Cedar and I are quiet as we take the trail away from the quarry overlook. The steps we take seem easy. Our breaths are small sighs. Soft sounds. They remind me that all is well; Frenchie has been found.

We are yards away from our car when I hear a branch snap, then a muffled whicker in the woods. I look, and my breath catches.

The piebald deer.

He is standing knee-deep in the soft brush, just off the dirt road. Head up, he sees us. He watches. His white patches seem bright as sunlight in the darkening woods.

"Stop," I whisper. Since I am in the lead, Mom and

Pop and Cedar freeze behind me. "On your left. See the deer?"

I hear my parents gasp.

"It's a piebald," I whisper. I turn slowly, look at Cedar and put my fingers to my lips. He smiles at me.

He whispers, "Bye-baw dee-yah."

We watch, still as stones. The piebald reaches up and snaps a clump of leaves off a striped maple. His antlers have grown out, pale and curled. He chomps, but he keeps looking at us. Like all the other times I've seen him, he doesn't spring—not right away—and I know we could get closer. I look for a way in. Suddenly, I see that we not alone. My heart starts pounding.

It's Jewell Laramie.

Hunter.

I see her orange vest, her rounded back. She is crouched and inching closer to the piebald deer. My brain makes a mad leap back to the day in our kitchen when she said the words, *clean double-lung shot.*

"No!" I run at her—fast as I can—knees high, needle-point purse flapping. I push my hand deep into my pocket. I close my fingers around my geode. I draw back my arm. Got my sights on a spot on the ground between Jewell and the deer.

"Ru-u-n!" I scream. I let the geode fly.

I trip and roll. Head over heels and finish flat on my back. There's a dizzying spin of light sky and black branches above me. Frenchie's purse is twisted around me. I close my eyes and cross my arms over my face. In seconds, Mom and Pop are beside me.

"Aurora! Oh, poor girl!"

And in the distance, I hear Jewell calling, "Aurora! Why, Aurora P.!"

Mom cups my forehead with her hand. "Are you all right? Open your eyes." But I can't, or I won't.

"D-did she hit him?" My voice shakes. "The piebald? Is he okay? Please, please . . ."

"He's gone," Jewell answers. I know she's right beside me now.

"Gone?" I think my heart will split.

"Well, you spooked him now, didn't you?" she says.

"So . . . you didn't shoot? With your bow?"

"Not on your life!" she says.

I open my eyes. Jewell is standing above me.

I roll onto my side and let out a moan. I press my face into my arm and rub my eyes. A few seconds later, I start to laugh—just a little. Then cry. Then laugh again. I don't know what to do with myself.

"I'm sorry, Jewell." I pull myself up to sitting. "But I thought you were going to shoot him, so I am *not* sorry too!"

"How about hurt?" Pop wants to know. "Are you hurt?" He pulls me to my feet and dusts a few forest crumbs off me.

"Yeah, that was an impressive tumble," Mom says.

"I'm fine," I say. "I didn't even feel it." I let out a laugh and smooth the needlepoint purse against my side.

"Jewell," I say, "are you okay?"

"I'm right as rain," she says. "May I say it? I appreciate that you didn't take me out with that pitch. I know you could have, kiddo. You, with your spectacular accuracy." She makes wide eyes at me.

"I figured I'd scare the deer away instead."

"Oh, so you thought about it?" Jewell teases. "Meanwhile, I hope you all got a good look at that magnificent creature. Whew! I have never seen anything like him, not with my own eyes, and I have spent my life in the woods. Dream come true for a woodswoman."

"For us as well," Mom says. "That spotted, speckled coat, and the way he looked back at us . . . leaves you with a sense of awe, doesn't it?"

"Rare treat on a rare evening," says Pop.

Then I tell them. "I've seen it before. More than once. So has Frenchie, and Cedar too. And I'll tell you something else, I think that's where Frenchie's been all this time, following that deer—and I know that sounds impossible. But the piebald doesn't scare as easy as most deer. I think the deer is the reason Frenchie walked away from school and why he never went home. Well, before he got trapped in the quarry, whenever that was."

"Why do you say so? What do you know?"

"I don't know anything for sure. But I've got a hunch,

315

and it's all because of Cedar." I look for my little brother, but he's making his way to the spot where the deer stood minutes ago.

"Because of Cedar?" Pop asks.

"Yep. He told me. No joking. In fact, he tried to tell us all. He's been saying *bye-baw* ever since yesterday morning. Today on the beach, I finally understood. Right before you came out to get us, Pop. Just before you told us Frenchie had been found. Cedar said, 'Enchie en bye-baw dee-yah.' Can you hear it?"

"Frenchie and piebald deer," Mom says with a nod.

"Beautiful!" Pop says.

"From the mouth of the babe!" says Jewell. "Why, little Cedar P.!"

"And . . . ," I say, "I even asked Carney Huggins if there was anything special about that deer he stopped for on Punkinville Road, and guess what?"

"The piebald." We say it together.

Cedar

What Cedar Petrequin Knew

Frenchie doesn't talk. He looks.

On Friday morning at the school, Cedar saw Frenchie looking out the car window. So he looked too. That's when he saw the piebald deer. The school was busy. Nobody was looking at the deer. Nobody but Cedar and Frenchie.

Cedar tried to tell Aurora. "Bye-baw! Bye-baw!" It sounded just right to him.

But she went along to meet her friends. Frenchie followed them into the school. Pop drove the car around the loop: stop and go, stop and go.

Cedar stuck one finger inside his ear where it ached. He twisted in his car seat so he could keep seeing the deer.

"Bye-baw!" He let out a cry.

"What's that you say, little buddy?" Up in the mirror, Cedar saw Pop's eyes.

"Bye-baw!" Cedar kicked and he cried and he pointed right at that piebald deer.

When Frenchie came out, Cedar saw him. Frenchie stood still. But when the deer walked away, Frenchie walked away with it.

Cedar tried to tell Pop. He tried so hard he cried. He caught a salty tear with the tip of his tongue.

Pop sang the railroad song.

So Cedar sang too. "Yidee yidee yidee-YAY-yo . . . ahh-dah yah-yah-YAY . . .." (It sounded right to him.) Singing made his ear feel better.

All along, Cedar Petrequin knew. Frenchie had followed the bye-baw dee-yah.

Aurora

Up Sundrop Meadow

I'm leading everyone up to Sundrop Meadow. Anzie Maylord invited us to come pick pumpkins, and we're taking her up on the offer. Cedar holds my hand, and we swing our arms. Leena and Joanie come along shoulder to shoulder. Frenchie keeps up fine, a few feet away.

Mom and Pop and Gracia are following. Close, but not too close. You can bet it'll be a while before any of us lets Frenchie out of our sight.

It's been two weeks since Mr. Menkis brought him up from that little ledge beside the quarry. He's looking like the same old Frenchie again: plaid shirt, khaki pants, belt tight. Needlepoint purse, full of bird prints, of course.

But I can tell you this: when Gracia brought him over

for breakfast the morning after the rescue, she told us, "He'll be all right, but he is very bruised." Saying it made her cry.

Mom hugged her around the shoulders for a long time.

Frenchie ate his pancakes standing up. Then he lay on his belly and studied his bird prints on our living room rug. It was four days before I saw him sit in a chair again. He's done a lot of healing. I've been watching. He doesn't look sore anymore. He walks the old Frenchie walk.

Today is a great day for a hike along the edge of the barrens. The little leaves on the blueberry bushes are a blaze of red, pink, and orange now. At Anzie's gate, we let ourselves in. We stand in front of the poem barn. This is new for Leena and Joanie. But Frenchie is ready. I can tell.

I begin to read—at the top of my lungs, of course.

SUN RAIN WIND SWEPT
BUD BLOSSOM BERRY

Leena and Joanie join in. The three of us shout the lines.

SWEET EARTH ROOTS KEPT
MAKE A SOUL MERRY

We're on a second chorus, and getting the giggles, when Carney Huggins comes out of the barn. He has both thumbs stuck into his ears. He waggles his fingers at us, sticks out his tongue, which makes us laugh even more. He tries to hide a grin but he can't, so he turns and runs back into the barn.

We try to get through the poem one last time. But one by one we drop to the ground because we're laughing so hard—and because we want to. Cedar lands beside me, legs in the air.

Only Frenchie is still standing. He's looking up, face to the sun. I prop on one elbow and wonder what he's thinking. But I don't have to know. I'll just keep on being here with him.

When he's ready he'll start heading home. He knows the way. That's Frenchie Livernois, my bird-loving, no-talk, very best friend.

Frenchie

That Same Day

Frenchie stood looking at the big white letters on the side of the barn, and he thought what he always thought when Aurora read them to him.

SUN SUN SUN.

Acknowledgments

I brim with gratitude every time my work goes to publication, never more than now. The world's challenges have been many; our strides have been necessarily long ones. We have adjusted and adapted. And I have never been more aware of how fortunate I am to be doing this work.

To my extraordinary editor, Katherine Tegen: thank you for the clarity you bring to our projects and, in this case, for helping me find the order of things. (The path through the puckabrush!)

Thanks to every good soul at Katherine Tegen Books and HarperCollins Children's Books for your hard work, dedication, and resilience in recent months, and for continuing to support me as you do. You are all deeply appreciated.

Thanks to Sara Schonfeld for good shepherding, and for helping me get the ever-changing-tree mural right. Thanks to your dad, the *near and dear* resource.

Miriam Altshuler, I am so proud that you are my agent. Your suggestion that the piebald deer belonged in a book took hold! Thanks for constantly doing your best by me.

Ramona Kaulitzki, thank for creating the lush and evocative cover art for this book as well as the gorgeous hand-drawn map on its interior. I love them both.

I have a bounty of good friends and family, who never let me stay lost on life's long, winding trail.

So, to my dear mom and dad, my siblings, my cousins and uncles and aunties, and the friends who are as close as family (all of whom seem to think I am way cooler than I really am), thanks for your endless love and encouragement.

To my critique group, *sheeshy-sheesh*, you are my rocks, my gemstones, my geodes, and my tourmaline! Thank you for always covering every detail with me.

To dear friend and writer, Sandi Shelton, another shining source of strength; my love and thanks for endless plot talks and plates of avocado toast.

I am ever grateful to prepublication readers Cammie McGovern and Eliza Factor (and Miranda too!) for their generosity and honesty. (See author's note.)

Mark Mendel, thank you for your poem barns and environmental art projects. For me, the Penobscot barn has served as the gateway to my annual summer writing retreat for twenty-five years. Always, it signals a beginning. (See author's note.)

Thanks to Obadiah Buell and Kelly Dean, for inviting me (and all visitors) to roam the stunning quarry and Granite Garden Gallery up on Whales Back Road in Sullivan, Maine.

To the piebald deer, thank you for showing yourself and staying a while. (See author's note.)

A mountain of thanks to you, my readers. Fact: there is no story without you. Doubt me? Well, consider that eternal question: If a tree falls in the woods and there's no one there to hear it, does it make a sound? The same applies to story.

Finally, to Jonathan and my kids, Sam, Kristy, Marley, and Ian: thank you for the love we share and the ways we celebrate it. (Dang, we are lucky ones!)

Author's Note

Anybody Here Seen Frenchie began with an unexplainable little seed that planted itself late at night. I was almost asleep when I sat up and reached for the pack of 3" x 5" cards I keep on my night stand. I wrote down two fragments:

flapping and tweeting

a bowl in the earth

When I looked back at my jottings in the morning light, I remembered what I'd seen in my mind's eye. It struck me that I'd found an ending. I felt a longing for the journey.

I had been thinking about a pair of middle graders who find in each other something both of them desperately need: friendship. In this case, it is a friendship nuanced by neurodiversity and the vastness of the autism spectrum.

I was determined to get these characters right, particularly Frenchie, who does not speak. With an early draft in hand, I turned to Cammie McGovern and Eliza Factor for comments based on their personal experiences raising autistic sons. Their firsthand insights were invaluable; they helped me to consider the complexity of loving an autistic person. (Eliza's daughter, Miranda, offered the sibling perspective as well.) I gave their reflections my full attention, and I believe with all my heart that Cammie and Eliza added depth, nuance, and authenticity to *all* my characters. If I've been successful, it's because of them; if I've failed, it's entirely my responsibility.

About the Poem Barn: This structure provided the inspiration for Anzie Maylord's poem barn. Created by artist and poet Mark Mendel in 1975, the barn with its

30' x 40' stenciled poem sits atop a favorite meadow of mine in Penobscot, Maine. Mr. Mendel's poem doesn't rhyme, whereas the one in the story does. I needed a poem that could also be a marching song for Aurora. Rhyme worked best. (Apologies to Mr. Mendel.) To learn more about Mark Mendel and his poem barns (there are more, but not enough in my opinion), please visit www.markmendel.com.

About the piebald deer: over a period of two years, my family and I delighted in repeated sightings of this piebald deer on the wooded land trust property adjacent to our house (part of his home range) in southern Connecticut. He is unforgettable. He stole my whole heart.

—Leslie Connor